GW00392830

The Chian Wine

and other stories

———◆◇◆———

Patrick O'Brian's success as a historical novelist and his distinction as a translator have made some people forget that he first established his reputation as a writer of short stories.

The present collection confirms his place in the front rank of contemporary short-story writers. His mastery is shown in the sheer excellence of the writing and the effortless variety of mood and tone. *The Virtuous Peleg* is enchantingly funny: *A Passage of the Frontier* and *The Chian Wine* in different ways exciting and terrifying; *The Rendezvous* and *On the Wolfsberg* quiver with disquiet. And nowhere in contemporary fiction have the passions aroused by field sports been better portrayed than in *The Curranwood Badgers*, *The Long Day Running* and *The Last Pool*. But of all the stories it is *The Handmaiden* that delivers most perfectly the concealed *coup de grâce* that only the master-craftsman can bring off.

Of the seventeen tales here printed, six appear for the first time. Nearly all the others have been extensively rewritten. The author is now at work on a biography of Picasso, to which he brings not only his gifts as a writer but the first-hand knowledge of the French, Spanish and Catalan background, physical, cultural and linguistic, that enriches the present book.

The CHIAN WINE
and other stories

———◆◆———

PATRICK O'BRIAN

COLLINS
St James's Place, London
1974

...illiam Collins Sons & Co Ltd
London · Glasgow · Sydney · Auckland
Toronto · Johannesburg

First published 1974
© Patrick O'Brian 1950, 1953, 1955, 1956, 1973, 1974
ISBN 0 00 221893 3
Set in Monotype Baskerville
Made and printed in Great Britain by
William Collins Sons & Co Ltd, Glasgow

For Mary, with love

Contents

———◆◆◆———

The Rendezvous

———◆◆◆———

CLEARLY umbrellas must often blow inside-out (how many times has one not had to tack violently in the turbulence at a street corner, grasping the mast with both hands and just, but only just, succeeding in dipping the rim under the current?) yet all my life I had never seen one. There it lay, a smallish umbrella, neither particularly a man's nor a woman's, in the shining, wet-running street, well away from the tumultuous gutter. It was not an old abandoned thrown-away umbrella – everyone has seen *them* – but a fairly new one: you could tell at first glance that it was malformed in some way, but it was not until you saw the metal ribs sticking through the respectable bright cloth that you understood it had been blown inside-out and that its defeated owner had made an attempt at folding it again before realizing that there was no hope and laying it deliberately in that position, parallel with the street, in nobody's way, relinquishing it kindly, perhaps with a certain respect.

One's eye takes these things in at great speed (I was running at the time), and all the faster if there is any sense of crisis, any amorous excitement or impending catastrophe: afterwards one's mind has to plod along rationalizing the eye's instant answer, its explanation of the problematical wreck, the overturned car, the domestic scene in a lit window as the train runs by. The sense of crisis was there, as well as the other factors, for the town was on the edge of disaster. The heavy rains of the last three days had been followed that morning by a stupefying downpour: warm rain hurtling down in drops of far more than natural size and between these drops a fine mist of shattered water. The earth could take up no more and already the river was a great cambered churning ochre mass from bank to bank, tearing furiously at the bridge, and by the Prefecture the orderly canal had drowned its trim brick walls, while the municipal oleanders, their roots ten feet below, jerked their highest leaves, their tallest twigs, among the filth and rubbish on the uneven, breakneck surface. And apart from the general crisis I had my own as I ran splashing past this umbrella. The Paris express would leave (if it were still running) in eight minutes: the station was a quarter of an hour away, and there was not a taxi to be seen anywhere in this flooded town.

There is something odious, almost unclean, in picking at oneself, slapping labels on to emotions and behaviour – peering through your own keyhole and perhaps at the same time putting on a show for the voyeur. However, there is no doubt a discreditable side to this perpetual missing of trains: and the running, the sweat (and how I sweated under my mackintosh in that steaming heat) only makes it more discreditable still. The cast-iron alibi, even to one's own court of conscience (but I *ran*, I ran all the way to catch it), grows less convincing in the hundredth repetition, particularly when it carries on into dreams.

Sweating and soaked I saw the express pull out and gather momentum as I burst from my last-minute cab. The red lights on the back of the last carriage swung round the curve and vanished – oh familiar nightmare – and I sheltered in the station buffet with its coffee-urns, its silent, frightened waitresses, the thunder of falling rain, sirens, apocalyptic candles in the gloom (the electricity had failed), the deep roar of running water everywhere.

However, by the time the next train left, the slow train, feeling its way over the flooded plains where only the embankment stood above the water – the vineyards all drowned – I was almost dry: though it was impossible to say the same for my book, or for her letter, or for the bundle of notes, of money (a source of great satisfaction to me) that I had thrust into my pocket for this rendezvous and that had soaked up the water to a surprising if not to a dangerous extent. And by the time I was in Paris the whole sky was blue – not so much as a cloud, not even on the southern rim.

I had already missed my connection and the essence of the rendezvous, of course: there could be no Cossack hat at the far end of the platform – did she still wear that hat, or had worms fattened on the Persian lamb? – no tall head stretching taller still behind the ticket-collector, no pale-blue eyes looking cold and remote until they flashed into recognition. Should we have shaken hands, kissed? Stood lumpish, undecided, muttering 'How well you look – not changed in the very least', each waiting for the other to make the spontaneous unstudied gesture, to define the relationship? Should I have been able to control my voice? That had haunted me ever since I opened her letter.

So I had missed the essence of the rendezvous; and as for telephoning in London, hearing that mortal 'ringing tone' in an empty flat, counting thirteen, counting thirteen again before hanging up, I could do that just as well from Paris. But there was still a train to Dieppe I could catch if I hurried, and at that juncture it seemed to me I ought to go through all the required motions. In that phoney histrionic voice which comes booming out when in fact far deeper real emotions are there below, I said it was right that I should die by inches in a call-box at Victoria rather than in an archaic booth at Austerlitz – that it should in common respect for her cost me two new pence rather than ten new francs.

This time I reached the train by racing through the barrier and although two doors would not yield I wrenched the third open and leapt in as the whistles blew and red flags waved. An empty compartment, smelling of dust, with views of Bayeux, Caen, a grisly watering-place, and three graffiti: *Couple criminel, vomi par la cité, faiseurs d'orphelins; Je t'aime, Nicole;* and *Vive moi.*

For the first quarter of an hour or so the railway from Paris to Dieppe perpetually crosses and re-crosses the river: you see it now on the one side and now on the other, and far off through the window a toy Eiffel Tower where you do not always expect it. It was while I was sitting in the carriage that I worked out this piece about the umbrella, its significance (shield, broken, carefully laid aside) and its obvious connection with missing trains; and when at about tea-time we stopped on a blank stretch of line I had little hesitation about getting out. Little hesitation, but still some: the sewing of my right-hand or should I say right-foot shoe, overtaxed by my paddling in it and by its stewing hours of heat in the waiting-room, had started to come undone. It was not so much that the sole had come frankly off, flapping downwards, as that the upper part had begun to rise; yet it seemed to me that by now the relative movement had stopped, and as I had always wanted to see this piece of river close to I opened the door and dropped on to the stones that make the permanent way: rough, pointed stones, flecked with oil and tar, of a kind to be seen nowhere else. It was an odd feeling to lay a hand on the lower edge of the tall train and to know that I was still in touch with it, that I could still become an integral part of it, and that if I chose not to do so it would move off, *exit left, gasping and heaving,* leaving nothing between this side of the line and the river but transparent air: at the bottom right-hand corner of the carriage, in gold on the brown background, stood the single word Purge.

The river was exactly as I had hoped it would be. There are so many places that can only be seen from a train – landscapes as absolute as the moon, railway-cuttings filled with cowslips, and grave-eyed badgers pacing there between them. Here was the broad Seine, full but not flood-full, rolling from brim to brim, and on my right, where Purge had been, the long spit of a tree-covered island coming to a point in the middle of the stream. A motor-barge pulling a string of lighters was thrusting up through the current towards the far side of the island, and on the near side a bright blue and red ship with the Belgian flag came floating down. It was a great wide view that I had, though not distressingly large – none of the dehumanizing expanse that you see from an aeroplane: perhaps two miles upstream to where the island merged into the general blur, and somewhat less to a curve that shut off the water in the other direction. Just before this curve I could make out a hard line that I believed to be a weir; and if I was right, then, oh joy, there would be five acres of detergent foam, and swans swimming in the Tide.

It was all that I could have wished. Warm, still, gentle, luminous air; a mild, veiled sun; the light brighter in some places than in others – Seurat near to, Claude Lorraine farther off. Before I moved the bow-wave of the motor-barge had vanished behind the island and a woman had hung out a line of bright washing on one of those that it towed. Some other vessels had come into sight here and there and not very far from the bank I could now make out the necessary fisherman, his heavy green boat moored against a background of reeds: but although there might be all this light and movement the whole effect was that of a uniform silence. Nothing that moved moved abruptly; there was the gliding continuity of the water and the swimming of the boats, and what human motion there was was small and doll-like in the distance. The angler never stirred.

I found the old tow-path and began to walk downstream, with the very agreeable sensation of being wafted along, of being part of the general flow. Of course, the sides of the path were somewhat overgrown, but a bare white track ran down the middle of it, and no doubt it would take me as far as Rouen if I let myself go with it long enough.

The hard line was indeed a weir, a weir that I knew well from the train, and it had its solid park of froth ending in a rounded point from which the current plucked islands and white ribbons, carrying them far down the river, out of sight; but no swans, except for a disappointing grey cygnet on the other side. This was an area I knew intimately well, from having gazed at it out of the windows of another world, but my knowledge was partial, based upon another sense of time and distance, and it did not extend to names. It did not extend to the great works with chimneys and open ironwork towers beyond the stream, either (I must always have looked too fixedly at the weir); but I was not surprised to see it, for there were many such things, vast inhuman enterprises that seemed to work themselves, spread out arbitrarily along this river. The drifting smell persuaded me that it was a chemical works; yet as far as I could see the world was unaffected by it. The chimneys bore their plumes of smoke, the unnatural reek came across the air; yet the river flowed and the trees stood up round and green, as though the two entities were entirely independent of one another. How different this will be, I said with a little skip, when I come to the burning fields.

But they were far away. First I had to follow the Seine round a noble bend that curved back on itself in a more than S, and this took me upwards of an hour: an S that the train annihilated by drawing a dollar stroke across it at eighty miles an hour. Dutch barges in the middle, with their flags; a very long low vessel with its body awash and a ridiculous wooden house perched up on one end – French; another Belgian, riding high with its screw churning white; yet not a sound did I hear until the very tail of the S, when a magpie flew from a bush on the left and trailed far out over the river, cackling as it went. Until then there might have been a deafness on the world.

Now for the first time plain agricultural land came down to the river on my side of it. Fields, divided by post and wire; leys; a fair amount of stubble, some of it already ploughed; neat heaps of dung; no people – just the fields and in one of them an empty cart. Another turn: meadows with lapwings calling over them, and along the river-bank (propped by piles, black baulks of timber, at this point where it was so deep) the tall dipping gallows of a row of fish-traps, archaic things like lateen masts, some with their baskets hoisted up, others dipping attentively. Beyond them lay an empty ferry-boat, moored to a wavering pier; and here a road came down to the river, a cart-track from a village or from the small collection of farms whose dark outbuildings I could make out behind a line of trees. Another mile, with an easy path under my feet; a few boats, and nothing else moving in the world except for one moorhen that jerked its neck among the reeds.

Now I was coming closer to my Sodom: already there were some sickly willows on the bank, by no means as sweet a green as those on the farther side, and a far greater profusion of the rank yellow weed called Stinking Willy. A train went by on the other bank, running at full stretch for Paris, and it gave me a pleasant feeling of being both here and there – a feeling slightly marred however by a lingering impression of guilt that I did not choose to identify at that moment; the association of trains and morose delectation, no doubt. The vegetation was thinning out; even the harsher kinds of grass had a stunted, lightless, sullen look; the naked earth showed more and more, a damp, soured desert; and here at last was my burning field. A great long rectangle, perfectly neat, perfectly level; and it was all made up of a black, coke-like substance, lying there in unspeakable profusion and emitting trails of smoke, yellow rising fumaroles, small pink flames here and there, and sometimes, where the smoke was darkest, a dusky crimson glow. No wire round it, no fence. No warnings: apparently no road. I had always wanted to smell it, and now, since the movement of the air was against me, I eagerly climbed from the towpath to the

15

first black crunching scoriae. I could not stalk about on
it as I had promised myself, because my gaping shoe
would let in some furious spark; but I did take a few triumphant paces, and immediately the heat rose up through my
soles.

Bare earth with a sulphurous efflorescence came next,
then sparse foul shrubs, twitch, and rose-bay willow-herb in
seed. Gradually the trees improved – taller, more sprightly.
Almost all traces of my burning field had gone by the time
I came to these allotments late in the day, these oblongs of
kitchen-garden huddled together, speckled with tool-sheds
made of old shutters, railway sleepers and metal advertise-
ments; a scene that could only be explained by the presence
of some industrial village hidden behind the rising land.

And now there were figures in the landscape, a group of
youths clustered strangely behind one of the little sheds.
They were near enough for me to see the black leather
jackets, the big shining buckles, the unmistakable hair, the
thickness of the frontal bone, the deep unluminous skin, and
the shot-gun that the tallest had in his hands. They broke up
on seeing me, some running, all moving rapidly away from
the bothie; then they slowed to an exaggeratedly casual
film-cowboy stride, with many an evil look backward. In
the first moment the group – they had certainly been breaking into the shed – had lost much of its cohesion, but by
the time they had passed through the remaining allotments
they had regained it, and with it all their bold inhumanity.
Their direction, as far as they had any direction, was down
the river, and for some minutes we all walked slowly
towards Rouen. Slowly, because that was their pace; and
slowly, because I had no wish to catch them up.

The river was beginning one of its smooth splendid
curves again, bearing away to the left, and this bend
enclosed a vast half-moon of marshy land, intersected by
palely shining ditches and a much larger reed-lined canal.
'I shall cut across the bend,' I said, 'for although there is

nothing against stepping out and passing through the midst of them, I do not choose to do so.' All lies, all lies, of course; there was everything against walking through the midst of them, for we were not indifferent; a relationship had already been established, and its rays were darting to and fro – fear, dislike and contempt on my side, and malignance, revolt and bloody dissatisfaction on theirs.

It was a great mistake, a bleeding error: I had none of the local sureness of a man of those parts, one who knew his way among the ditches and whose knowledge would have given him an assured countenance even through the back of his head. I had hardly begun my uncertain blundering through the reeds before I turned from a spectator to a quarry.

There was no overt move for a little while and indeed the knowledge of the situation did not spread to all minds and to all levels of awareness without a considerable delay. Besides there was a gap in time, a parenthesis, in which they shot a magpie (they shot at everything that moved), winged it, and thrashed about after it as it ran, hopped and fluttered, sometimes, poor bird, skimming to a moment's safety in the reeds on the far side of a broad ditch.

But soon enough there I was, going faster and faster along my predetermined chord while one straggling line of youths hurried shouting along the towpath and another, more compact, launched out across the marsh on a course that would intercept mine unless I either ran or deviated to the left. I deviated, all right. My chord became a curve, and the curve sharpened sensibly as the gleam of gun-barrels in the fading light caught my eye. At some point, unseen by me, the sun must have sunk into a band of haze low over the trees beyond the river, and now the white light of the evening was shining from all the water in the bog. Steadily on, with the marsh-smell rising to my nose and the marsh-mud (viscous, dark) packing into the gap between the sole and upper of my shoe, working under the arch of my foot.

On, on. What dreadful galvanic energy possessed those youths, what superabundant activity, unnecessary life!

In front of me stretched a surface far wider than I had expected: this was the canal that drained the middle of the bog; and it looked very deep. Some ditches I had leapt, without too great an air of flight (I thought) and some I had crossed on planks. But here was no bridge that I could make out, and if I were seen attempting to jump it – it might just be done – then there would be no disguising the situation. The leap would be an open acknowledgement that the thing had turned into a hunt and myself into a legitimate prey. Besides, I did not know which side of the canal they were: they might have crossed it by the bridge that must certainly exist at the far end, where the canal fell into the Seine. Staring round did me no good, for here I was among the reeds, and their feathery heads cut off my view. An irresolute step took me away to the left along the canal, and here, just past a low-spreading willow-tree, there rose up an enormous shape. Straight up into the air it rose and after a stab of pure terror I recognized the broad wings and shape and colour of a heron: at once the shape diminished to a natural size. The slow beating flight rose and turned into the evening breeze from the river, mounting languidly, as herons will.

Then came the double bang-bang of the gun and the heron slanted down in a long glide towards the river-bank. There was a confused shouting and bellowing of orders, raucous, ugly, near-hysterical, and then another shot. I made my way fast along the canal, keeping down among the reeds and the willows, and at length I paddled my way into a particularly dense clump of bulrushes that stood around a little sub-sidiary pond. Here I squatted on a tussock of that wiry grass which stands dry in the wettest places. There was the best part of the shell of some bird's egg under the tussock next to mine, and one could still see the bent-lined hollow in which it had been laid. 'Tranquillity,' I said; and I noticed that the light was too dim to make out the colour of the shell. To some degree I was still unwilling fully to admit that I was hiding; but in reply to the commonplace observation 'these things just don't happen – you are upset, nervous, all on edge' my memory produced details of gratuitous acts of this very nature and repeated them over a long period. And when I heard movements and voices again in front of me – that is to say further along the canal than the point I had reached – my whole being at once acquiesced and compressed itself into a smaller space, eyes glaring, ears and nostrils stretched: no doubt it also emitted a quarry's smell. And I was surprised to find my hand creeping towards my wad of notes: I had not consciously thought of them since the train, so very long ago. There was the faintest wetness still to be detected in their heart.

'There! In there!' shouted a voice, and someone threw a clod of earth into the rushes and the water: but it was twenty or thirty yards away. Still, this full admission was very bitter, and beneath the humiliation I felt a surly glow begin to rise.

It might have grown into something very rough and careless in time or with a sudden emergency, but it had certainly not reached that point yet, and I lay as close as a hare. As far as I could tell they were scattered promiscuously over the marsh – some of them shouting a great way off – and they seemed to be skirmishing about in twos and threes. What I could not make out was where the gun might be.

Nor, when at last I came out of my hiding-place, could I make out which way round I was. West I could tell, for there was the remaining yellow glow; but the closer lie of the land escaped me – the canal no longer seemed to be running in the right direction, and the chess-board ditches (as far as they could be seen at all in this dying glimmer, faintly helped by a weak-backed moon) had been slewed round so that they no longer pointed out my way. There were a few voices still to be heard, mostly quite far off. They no longer had the fierce zeal of the earlier stage, but still I went on cautiously, working in what I thought was the direction of the river; and when I heard a cry of 'Look out! There he is!' I turned at once.

The frightened tone was cordial to me, so was the sight of shadowy figures fleeting away from me over the marsh; but still I edged off into cover, since they might be running straight to their friends.

Now there was a great deal of that foolish ululating oo-ooh that townspeople keep up so in the country: but quite commonplace now, none of that implacable passionate intensity that you hear when hounds hit off the line – silly human beings was all. And I supposed, as I sat on my heels in a hollow, that they had gathered again, at least into two bands; though there was some isolated whistling and bawling over to the left.

The weak moon had gathered spirit: it had put out the Pleiades and it shone on every watery stretch. A heavy dew was falling: wet piled upon wet.

'If only I had a piece of string,' I said, 'how much easier it would be.' My sole was now a true drooping sole. I had to raise my foot six inches higher than I should ordinarily have done, to prevent it from stubbing on the ground; and at every step I grasped with my toes – a useless, unnecessary, and (after a thousand repetitions) a very tiring action.

My direction was unsure – quite vague. I had thought of making my way back to those allotments and thence to my hypothetical village, but on reflexion I preferred the towpath, and it seemed to me that if I kept on a general westerly course I must come to it in the end. It must surely be over there; and yet here was a metalled road, a meaningless road, if ever I had seen one. What was my right course now? On the far side, beyond still another ditch, stood a sign-post. I could have sworn that even a newspaper would have been legible in this brilliant moon – at least the headlines – but

when I walked across (the road-grit sharp under my
ridiculous foot) I found that I could not make out a single
word. By now I was not going to leap another ditch with my
shoe in that shape merely to learn, perhaps, that I might not
deposit ordure there, so I considered for a while; and seeing
that the road seemed to slope a little to the right, I went
down it: in a quarter of a mile it brought me to a raised
bank, and as soon as I had walked over it there was the
Seine, there were the lights of some great installation far
over on the other side, and between this bank and that
two boats crossing on the black water. They hooted gently
to each other as they passed, and their washes crossed
reciprocally, the ripples showing in the light. The river was
flowing the way I had expected it to flow – how comforting
– and where I stood the metalled road ended in a gravelly
place with a small ferry, just large enough for a single car.
And here was the towpath: I started along it – so much
easier than the broken surface of the bog, and presently the
whole ludicrous, painful incident, which had already
diminished wonderfully, dwindled into a foolishness long
past.

It did not revive even when my mind was jerked from its
mild inward rambling by a sound that it told me was caused
by a bullock churning about in a wet pasture, frightened by
its own shadow. But it did revive in all its full strength, it
did shock my heart to a momentary halt and wring my
stomach tight again when I saw the youth bolt upright by
the mast of a fish-trap. The moon was shining full upon him.
Was he dim-sighted, half-witted, a nyctalope, to suppose
himself invisible? Had he read in a book that if you stand
quite still you cannot be seen?

Quite still he stood, and as I came closer I could see the
moon shining blue upon his teeth – a black hole of mouth
and then these teeth. In that light his face seemed drained,
eyeless, and sweating cold, for what could be seen did also
glisten.

My foot had made the smallest pause when I saw him, hardly measurable it was so small, because I knew that the entire situation was reversed, utterly reversed; and I came on with my awkward lame-duck gait.

'Have you a piece of string?' I said.

No answer. No movement. The line of barges that had been following me passed by and I saw him silhouetted against the navigation lights.

'Have you a piece of string?'

His eyes showed in the moonlight, a sudden gleam (had they been closed?), and in an abrupt harsh rush he said, 'Yes, a whole ball of string. A whole ball of string. Twine.'

'Why does he carry a whole ball of twine with him?' I wondered as I sat down. I said, 'What is the name of the next village?'

'Bougival,' he answered gently, very soft.

'Bougival,' I said, seeing the map quite clearly now. 'Ah, Bougival. Why, yes, of course, it must be Bougival, the place where lettuces are grown. I shall telephone from there.'

The Valise

———◆◆◆———

IN THE COUNTRY around this village it is not as simple as one could wish to find a pleasant, easy path for walking. The roads inland are all uphill, and although it is true that they lead through magnificent, dramatic country – bold, falling rock with terraces of vines and olive trees standing among the dried-up, barren mountains – they are roads that have to be climbed with attention: the landscape makes continual demands upon one; the winding, rock-strewn paths need perpetual care, and both these things interfere with the real aim of a walk, which for me is a half-conscious gentle physical exercise, the perfect accompaniment to reflection. I do not say that the countryside is anything but superb, and for one who walks to see magnificence these paths are ideal: but that is not my aim, and sometimes I long for an ordinary sober country lane, a way through the level cornfields or a towpath along a quiet river or a sea wall between salt flats and a marsh. Then there is the heat: for a big, heavy man that is important, and in the summer (it lasts from April to November here) all these roads are tilted to the blazing sun throughout the day.

The alternative is to walk along the sea. It is fresher in the summer, but there again it is not the kind of walking that I like best, for the sea is bordered by high cliffs: the sea comes right to their feet, and there is no way along the shore; one must be climbing or descending all the time.

When I was a little boy I lived for a time in a place where there was an immense stretch of sand; hard, pounded sand upon which you could walk for miles and miles. You never

23

had to watch your feet on the level sand: walking was effortless, and the rhythm of your steps and the half-heard incessant thunder of the sea induced that trance in which one can go on and on for ever, singing perhaps, or preaching to the stones. There were shells, too, far better than the shells are here, delicately stranded at the watermark, and all kinds of sea-wrecked things, trawlers' floats, kelp, sea purses, spindrift, tarred or whitened planks of wood.

That is the sort of strand that is lacking here; for here, as I say, there is no way along the sea except by the cliffs, and although they do sometimes go down to a little bay of shingle, it is only to rise again abruptly within a hundred yards. It is not a coast for general wandering: it is not a shore where one can stroll at all, and that is my only complaint against this place. I have no others. My lodgings are clean and orderly, the people are used to me, they are quiet and civil, and nobody interferes with my work or my set habits.

However, there is one walk that is neither violent nor exhausting. It is not a very good walk: it is an illogical, synthetic walk, but it is the best that I have been able to find and I have gone over the paths of it so often now that my feet find their way by themselves, leaving my mind free, to meditate or drift in vacancy, just as it pleases; and that is all that one can ask.

I go out of the back of the village, past the fort: this is a bad part, for the quarter's rubbish-heap is by the fort, and there is always a carrion smell and the thin dogs hunt about in shameful, mean-looking bands. The rubbish is supposed to be burned in that square concrete box, but although a cloud of stinking smoke drifts over it, the amount is never the less. I pass it and hurry over the bare drying-ground: the wind is almost always in the right direction, and as soon as I am on the level field the reek is blown away, so by the time I am halfway over it the unpleasant feeling has quite gone. This is the place where the women spread their washing out to dry, and in certain months of the year the men bring their nets to lie in the sun.

Beyond the drying-field one must branch off to the left, to the main road and follow it to the entrance of a broad cart track: this is where the walk begins. The track dips down between high banks, and very soon there are hedges on either side. These are the only hedges for miles around, and if it were not for the prickly pears that show here and there and the pomegranates that form part of the hedge itself, one might suppose the track an English lane. On the far side there are orange-trees and vines, which destroy the effect, but all around the farmhouse that stands on the downward slope an ordinary market garden gives the green in ordered rows again – broad beans, cauliflowers and cabbages, lettuce, carrots, familiar plants. Farther down, the bushes close overhead and the lane becomes a tunnel through the green; then at the bottom there is the river. For nearly all the year the bed is dry, and even when there is some water flowing it is always possible to cross dry-shod. Now I turn to the right and follow the path downstream. Here there are laurels, a few willows, tamarisks and those tall, thin bushes that have purple sprays of flowers – the kind that bloom in the late summer and draw flights of peacock butterflies.

Among the bushes there are dragonflies, for the river, flowing underground, leaves stagnant pools in the hollows: and up and down the river-bed, low under the trees, innumerable swallows dash through the light; there are martins, too, and in the evening when the bats are out and the swallows are no more than dark blurs, more sensed than seen, the white bottoms of the martins show, disembodied, weaving up and down.

I follow the river then, and come to its mouth. This is in one of the little bays that I have mentioned: it stands between the cliffs on either hand, a half-moon of shingle, with tall reeds at the back of it and behind them an orchard of fig and orange trees. The river, when it is flowing, hugs the right-hand side, cutting along at the foot of the cliff itself, and the beach shows no sign of having a river in it at all.

It is a shingle beach, with large pebbles at the back and small ones by the sea. Nearly always there is a high-water-mark of broken reeds, bushes, driftwood and grass-like seaweed: this line of vegetable rubbish (it is as much as two feet high sometimes) stays unmoved from one big storm to another. Only at the equinox, when the wind comes straight in from the sea, do the waves beat in so far, and then there is nearly always rain inland, so that the river brings down more dead reeds and bushes, and these, being unable to drive out to sea, drift in the little bay and are thrown in to the same high-watermark.

It is only at these times, too, that the one boat that lives on that beach is hauled up far from the sea. It is a blue boat, shaped like those one made from paper as a child; the old man of the orchard uses it to fish for congers. He spends more time in his boat than working on his land, and it is said that he knows the rocks at the bottom of that bay better than most men know the rooms of the house they live in. But he is a savage old man, a solitary, and I do not speak to him nor he to me.

When I am on the strand I usually walk up and down it. It is not that it is agreeable to walk upon – the shingle is so loose and shifting that one's feet plunge deep and walking is painful – but it is the end of my walk. One must either go back the way one came (an unsatisfactory retreat) or else climb up the cliff, which is not *walking* any more. It is the cliff path that I nearly always take, up past the destroyed German searchlight and to the huge domed gun-emplacements home; but I walk up and down first to consider it.

I walk, naturally, by whatever watermark there may be. Not the high ridge-like mark of the great storms, for that so rarely changes, but by the sea itself; and sometimes, when there has been a swell, or a storm in Africa, there are shells or wreckage on the beach.

Once I found a wet brass ring. It had just arrived from who knows what rolling in the sea. It was a cheap ring, the kind that is sold in fairs: the sea had pitted it with eatings-out and dents, which gave it the look of vast antiquity. But in low relief on the flat part of it there was a swastika, and no doubt it had belonged to one of the Germans drowned here in the war. The ring filled me with repulsion, like a thing unclean: the round was so much the answering shape to the finger that had fitted it that I shuddered and threw it far into the sea, wiping my hands on the pebbles afterward. A human finger, by itself without a hand, is a disgusting thing. A human finger in the sea.

The pelvis that I found did not have the same effect. This was not long after the ring, and it lay within a yard or two of the same place: but I did not connect it with the Germans drowned – nor, indeed, with mankind at all.

It was by itself, white, dry and smooth, symmetrical and polished to inhumanity by the sea. It was only by a conscious effort that I could feel that this had been a piece of a man – only by running my hand round my own hip to my spine and tracing the same rise and curve that I saw on the bleached and diagrammatic bone in front of me. It had been in some way human, that was true; but is a shell the shellfish? This pelvis was very like a shell. Ordinarily, I suppose, a human bone would raise some emotion, some emotion resembling piety; it would be a disturbance of decency, a kind of profanation on the shore. But I felt no such emotion as I sat looking at this bone: I connected it with death, but with no particular death. A specimen in an anatomical museum could more easily have been clothed with living flesh than this white basin in the sun.

One's mental processes, and especially the wandering fantasies that pass through one's mind as one walks, are linked by a chain of association so slight that it usually cannot be traced. The thorns of a bramble will claw out from a thicket: one pushes on automatically, and then in half an hour one will find that one has been dwelling on the Passion for the last mile of the road. That is why I speak of this bone: it provides the obvious and unfortuitous start for the recollections that unfolded in my head as I walked up the cliff path and high along the edge of the sea to the ruined batteries, where the camouflaged concrete still lies among the thistles and the asphodel, with its reinforcing steel rods all standing like the prickles of some prodigious monster of the earth.

When first I came to this village I lodged in a house belonging to an elderly couple named Joseph and Martine Albère. It was a large house, but I was the only lodger: a tall, gaunt place, always cold and damp, even in the height of the summer, and from the outside you would have said that it was uninhabited. But it was in good repair, a solid, middle-class house, much richer than the terrace-cottages in which most of the villagers lived: only the presbytery and the doctor's house were better; and from this I judged that the owner would be a man of some standing in the village. I learned, too, that my landlord was the owner and the equipper, the *armateur*, as they say, of three fishing boats: his boats, then, were the direct means of livelihood for nearly forty of the men of the place – a considerable proportion of the working inhabitants.

However, I soon gathered the impression that Albère was not a man of high standing. It is difficult to say how one forms an impression of this nature: it is built up of so many little things – gestures, tones of voice, a look cast backward, an avoiding eye – but in the end it grows into certainty. On the concrete, demonstrable side there was the fact that he never ran for municipal office, that he was president of none of the many co-operative or political associations and that he never appeared at any of the funerals or public feasts.

He seemed to be rich but unconsidered: a contradiction of common experience. At one time I asked myself whether in fact he was rich. Would a rich man take in a lodger? He did not seem to like letting the room I had; but when upon some trifling disagreement (he did not allow his lodgers the front door key) I suggested that I should find a room elsewhere, he showed so much concern that I could not but suppose he was in earnest. He at once proposed a much lower rent if I would give up my point, and after a little more discussion I agreed to stay. This caused him a disproportionate satisfaction.

Then I learned that he had a fourth boat building on the stocks, which disposed of my idea that he was poor, for at that time a new boat was a very costly undertaking. As for the letting of rooms, that might indicate much or little: after all, in a big house one might let rooms to keep the house lived in, simply to prevent that decay that always comes in an empty place.

But still he remained a curious man to me. He did not like me, and he did not like having me in the house: yet he did not want me to leave it. The rent that I paid was a trifle to him even before he reduced it, yet he forced himself to be amiable to me, provided my room with the meagre best of the furniture in the house, and waited up every night to let me in after my evening walk.

He was a small, dark man, about sixty-five years of age: he was always carelessly dressed, dirty and unshaved, and his air of brutality contrasted strangely with the house he lived in. How did this brutal air appear? He was not obviously vicious: he spoke politely enough to me (though it was patently constrained) and I can only say that it must have been his lurching walk, the set expression on his face and the way he terrorized his wife that made me think, 'Albère? A brutish man.' His wife I hardly saw: she was utterly effaced, and she moved about the darkened house furtively, with the sound of a person who is trying to make

29

no noise – this was when she was going about her obvious, everyday duties. She was much more like an imprisoned servant than the mistress of the house. Whenever she spoke to me he would appear and, whatever she was saying, she would stop and hurry downstairs. Yet I had the impression that in spite of this domination they were allies. Sometimes, in the dead quiet of night, I would hear them talking, two whispers, urgent and hurrying, that would answer one to the other in the basement of the house. They slept in the kitchen, and I do not think they ever used any other room.

When I had been there some time I learnt something of their habits. They did not sleep very much, and every few hours one or another of them (or sometimes both) would creep up to the top of the house, along the passage that traversed its length, opening every door softly and softly closing it again, then down the stairs to the middle landing, very silently past my door to the room beyond, and there they would pause, perhaps for as long as half an hour, before coming out, crossing quietly to the other side of the house, up the little stairs, through the garrets, back and down the breakneck flight to the hall, and so to their kitchen.

But I have my nocturnal habits, too: and more than once I have been there before them, fixed silent in a corner just off their trodden beat (for their patrol was so settled by long routine that their feet stepped in exactly the same places night after night), silent and unbreathing, watching their shadows.

However, this was much later: at first I merely noted that they never left the house together, and that when one was gone the other always waited in the hall or near it to open the door.

They appeared to have no relations. At least nobody ever came to visit them; and as far as I could see they were always in the house except when Albère was on the beach, conducting his business with the crews of his boats or when the woman was out for shopping. She never went to church: nor, of course, did he.

I had been there a long time before I found out what was the matter with them. It was a long time, for there were two difficulties in my way: the one was that the people of the village were not unduly open – they may know for generations, but they will not go out of their way to tell strangers – and the other, that I do not talk readily either. I do not go to cafés nor make acquaintance with the loungers on the quay. My form of recreation after my work is to walk. I like to go for long, uninterrupted walks.

Eventually it was a Dutch painter who told me what I had to know. He was a fat, exuberant man – spoke the language perfectly, having been brought up in Rheims – and he almost forced himself upon me. All he wanted was an audience: he loved to talk, and the smallest word of attention would keep him talking on the quay for hours. He was not my idea of a Dutchman. He knew all the fishermen and all the shopkeepers: he was hail-fellow-well-met with all of them before he had been here a month, and he stayed for a long time. It was a local man who told him about Albère: or perhaps 'local man' is inexact, for he was a waiter who had married a local girl and settled down here: he did not have the same sense of a closed community. The facts were common knowledge, and I often came across references to them afterward. Albère was originally a sailor, a seaman employed on the packet-boats that run between France and North Africa. On his ship, the *Jules-Bastide*, there were two other men from this village.

One night, about thirty years ago, the *Jules-Bastide* put out from Marseilles in a black gale of wind: there were very few passengers, for it was mid-winter, and most of those few went straight to their cabins. Only a few Algerian deck-passengers huddled on the fo'c'sle; and one solitary priest, indifferent to the weather, stayed on the afterdeck. He carried a black valise wherever he went. When he went below for dinner he kept it with him, and afterwards, when he returned to the deck in spite of the wild seas, he carried it still. He paced up and down in the gale, always carrying this valise. There were three men on duty on this part of the ship at this particular time, Albère and his two fellow-villagers.

In the morning the priest was missing. Nobody knew anything about it: the official inquiry revealed nothing whatever. There was even some mystery about the identity of the priest, as there had been a mistake in the list of passengers, and the person who had arranged for the priest's ticket could not be traced.

Shortly afterward the three men left the sea. One bought a café in the town ten miles up the coast; the second took an important farm some way inland; and Albère bought the house where I was staying and the three fishing boats.

Within a year the first man and his wife were burned alive in a fire that destroyed their house and café. Two years later the second man, already overcome by misfortune in all his enterprises, lost his only son: the boy was killed riding a motor-bicycle that his father had bought for him. The man returned to this village by foot, walked to the graveyard, and hanged himself in the daylight.

Ever since, the Albères had been waiting for their turn. They had taken me in as some kind of protection (the lightning, they thought, would not strike a house where a just man lived) but still they did not think that my presence was enough: they were still in dread, and I remembered how one night, early in my stay, I had gone out about three in the morning (I had thought it might be the beginning of the day of wrath, but when I looked at the stars I found that I was wrong) and I had unbolted the door without a sound. When I came back and closed it after me, I heard the stifled gasp that Albère made as he stood silently behind the door, and in the moonlight from the landing window I saw that he had a gun. He muttered something about thieves, but, as I thought at the time, you shoot thieves down. Thieves had their hands cut off in former days; they were also stoned to death. Some thieves were nailed and hung up alive.

Nothing has ever given me a livelier pleasure than my realization that they had taken me in as a protection. And it came to me quite slowly, as I was walking by the river, that once again I had been chosen as the hand of God. After such a long time it had come again: all my anxious waiting was rewarded. The wickedness of my doubt was overlooked – for at times I had wavered – and now once again I was the elected vessel. I had hoped for so long: and to hope for such an election more than thrice in one lifetime seemed presumptuous indeed. But now I was the hand of God again; the wrath of a jealous God Who spoke through the prophet and ploughed the Amalekites into the ground. And without any knowledge I had been set there in my place for a long year past: oh, it was the sweetest realization in the world, this kindness vouchsafed to me.

I waited for the dream that should direct my hand. It had been so clear and explicit before the whores of Coleraine, a pure, loving voice; even more so before the sawing of the blasphemer at Newtownards.

But it did not come at once this time, for in my lightness of spirits I could not sleep. And on that dear Thursday when Saturn moved into Capricorn my presumptuous unregenerate human will (I mean the Enemy), told me that I did not need further guidance now – that hesitation was a sin – that they were already delivered into my hand – that I was now to enjoy the reward for all my waiting.

The shadow of a salutary doubt still lingered in my mind that night when I heard them on the broad upper corridor between half past three and four o'clock; but the spirit of wantonness was so strong in me that I could not resist the pleasure. Once they were in the far room, listening, I threw my black coat over my nakedness and stepped out, barefoot. Not a sound.

They took a turn about the room, opening cupboards, and crept out: but I was there, fast in the shadow by the door, and as they came I sprang on them shrieking 'The priest, the valise, the priest, ha ha ha ha ha ha ha.' I leapt and I sprang, and with the shrieking and the laughter I could hardly run as fast as they did. They were some way ahead, the man before the woman, and I am bulky, heavily-built; but the man stumbled in front of the woman and with a bound I cut them off at the head of the stairs and hunted them into the room at the other end: I howled and howled in that room. After a while I let them escape by the far door and up the little staircase to the garrets – through and through the garrets (they ran silently) down to the second floor and up again and there I left them while I ran to leap and shriek all through the house.

Coming out of the parlour I sensed them creeping towards the upper landing: I raced up the little stairs behind, and there they were, a floor below. The man had the woman by the arm – they were trying to reach the door. The laughter almost choked my breath, but from up there I flew – I say I *flew* – and howled as I flew, striking the stair behind them.

How they fell I cannot say, but fall they did; and when I had finished on the landing there they lay, far down on the stone flags of the hall. To be sure, I did go and squat by them for a while; but even before I began to walk down that last flight I knew it was over – not half an hour and already it was over: only one bout and it was over.

It was over, and barely a mark on them: certainly not the clear mark of the Beast: and when they were cold I stepped into the kitchen – I always take a little refreshment before retiring: warm, watered milk for the sake of my sleep.

Sleep came at once, and with it, oh with it, my dream, as clear as a trumpet: I was to buy a shipbuilder's nail a cubit long from Albère's yard, said the voice: I was to hunt them into every room in the house and then into the cellar. I was promised more than ever I could have believed, if only I had waited for guidance: after a nightlong ecstasy I should have driven home the nail, not once, not once, but twice!

The Stag at Bay

---◈◈◈---

EDWIN, as the long and briefless years trailed on, devoted himself more and more to lecturing and journalism. At the moment he was labouring over an article on marriage for a women's magazine – 'Let it be chatty and smart. And rather profound – *human*: you know what I mean? And you can be wistful if you like: old, battered, experienced. But not more than fifteen hundred words.'

The article was proving much more difficult than he had expected. It was not for lack of raw material – pinned to the wall in front of him was a list of smart things that had already been said about marriage – and it was not for lack of experience or thought. Marriage was a subject that he had thought about a great deal, deeply, and he had supposed that the profound part of the article would be the easiest: yet although he was in the right mood, costive and solemn, the words would not form themselves into an orderly and harmonious procession. They remained in his head, swirling in grand but indeterminate shapes; or if they had any concrete existence at all it was in the form of scrappy notes, odd words jotted down: *marriage iceberg – sunk – top quarrels – corruption in state.*

Not from lack of experience: he was married himself and at this time he felt more than usually married, for not only was he immersed in this article, but Julia had left him again, had gone back to her mother, and he was conscious of this all the time, if for no other reason than that the place was in such a mess. He never cleared it up on these occasions, partly on what he called principle and partly because it gave him such a moral advantage to be found in a slum, with every crock and pot unwashed and dishes piled on the floor, bed unmade, laundry sprawling abroad. He would not deliberately make a hole in his sock; but he would not prevent it, either. And yet he would not consciously welcome the hole; he would say tut-tut over it and inspect it with distaste: still less would he acknowledge that he piled the dishes in an unnecessarily picturesque confusion. His recognition of his moral advantage took place on some remote and not very savoury level of awareness: the piling of the dishes was traditional in the helpless male – any comic strip would bear that out, and besides there was the principle Man works not in House – and it was quite unconscious when it was quite fair: it was quite fair of course because Julia was in the wrong; therefore it was totally unconscious.

Marriage iceberg. Somewhere he had read that seven-eighths of an iceberg is always submerged and that it is only the remaining eighth that one sees; and this he meant to liken to marriage, the visible berg corresponding to the squabbles and superficial disharmony and the vast unseen majority serving as a figure for the profound unity and deep affection that must always subsist, etc. A church-going expression covered his face: he nodded gravely, and bending over his desk he began to write.

His pen stopped, started again, faltered and limped: he crossed out the whole paragraph and began afresh. He must make it quite plain about the underneath of the iceberg being really there.

Slow, slow. The cat, which standing at the door had asked three times to go out, now paced deliberately into his bedroom.

It was a slow article to write. Julia had slammed the door behind her just after the smart pieces had all been collected and as the first words were being written, 'We all know Mr Punch's advice about marriage . . .' Yet the first section, the chatty part, had scarcely been completed before she had given Edwin grounds for divorce, and she was not by habit a flibbertigibbet, a fly-by-night, an itching palmer; neither loose nor fast. Her motives had been mixed: sizzling vexation of spirit, a conviction that nothing mattered; but also curiosity. She wanted to know, to really know, what adultery was like.

The article was still bogged down in the second, or human, part when, pursuing her research with an ardour that could no longer be attributed to revenge or a spirit of inquiry, she increased his grounds to a most liberal extent – to expansive and park-like grounds in which the horned beasts could be seen wandering at large.

At the beginning of the profound section she was in bed with horrible old Anthony Limberham, her cousin, to whose busy prayer she had yielded at three o'clock on Tuesday afternoon. She was quite accustomed by now to his faintly incestuous sheets – to their moral significance, that is – but not to the flagrant luxury of their hem-stitching, nor to the sinful depth of the carpet that met her feet when she got up. The unashamed magnificence of Anthony's flat, his delighted pursuit of the sins of the flesh, the huge and beautiful meals (no shopping, cooking, washing-up) they both ate so greedily, the flowers, the scent, the lovely clothes, all these refreshed her soul like rain after drought. She sloughed the anxiously contriving housewife, dropped ten years from her appearance, and responded to his cheerful obscenity with an assured impudence that no longer shocked her inner mind. Her eyes shone; she looked pink, virginal and inviting; her hair curled naturally; in all her life she had never felt so well.

Her sense of fun, much discouraged by life with Edwin and the hundred best books on the seventh floor of a cold-water walk-up, came suddenly to life again, and Anthony, scarlet in the face and wheezing, watered it with gin. She was going to the dogs – such agreeable dogs.

In the morning the tide of washing-up reached Edwin's desk

itself, and at eleven a little congealed bacon-fat obscured his views on the state. These views had got into the article because they seemed to him to follow naturally after the piece about icebergs: he had expressed them forcibly, at some length, and with particular feeling today. He found them satisfactory and comforting even now, although the bacon-fat had reduced them to a kind of aphoristic précis: '. . . corruption in state, however bad, always occurs over basis of working integrity – unseen, unheard, taken for granted. – Crime not crime if normal; and once it becomes normal, unthinkable dissolution of the state.'

Scraping some of the grease off with the paper-knife he commended himself for not being angry. He thought of ringing up his mother-in-law's house and telling Julia that she was forgiven: he thought of clearing everything away completely. But he sickened at the prospect of the actual effort; and then it really would be too Quixotic to throw away so much advantage. Magnanimity had its limits: and after all he had not been . . .

What exactly had he meant to forgive her for? His memory, usually so very precise in such matters, could not supply the grievance at once, and even after bungling about among the files for some time it could come up with nothing better than general disrespect, inattention, or answering back. There was no heinous crime, like the unmended drawers of the last great row. The prefect-Edwin was inclined to mercy; fright and the possibility of dismay were beginning to creep through the levels of consciousness and he was growing less absolute. But there was such a great deal of washing-up.

'Or we have a very fine oryx, sir,' said the shopman.

They looked thoughtfully at the noble, leaping symmetry of the polished horns. 'No,' said Anthony, after a moment, 'What I really want is a stag, and, to be precise, a royal with at least twelve points.'

'Don't be pedantic, Anthony,' murmured Julia, with a blush. She turned away and gazed under the arm of a polar-bear at the hurrying traffic. '. . . a long way before you find a royal, sir. We used to see them often in the old King's time, but now I'm afraid you'll have to go a long way . . .' the shopman said, bowing them out.

A long way, a long way, but they found it at last in the limbo of an auctioneer's back room.

'A very fine 'ed, if I may say so,' said the warehouseman, hurr-ing on the stag's eye and shining it with his handkerchief: it gleamed, brilliant among the dust and cobwebs that veiled the long muzzle, as bright and expectant as a natural in a bus. 'A very fine 'ed, sir,' repeated the warehouseman, polishing the other eye, 'And I dare say it was his pride in his days of life.'

He stood aside to watch Anthony, who had borrowed a clothes-brush, and who was busily grooming the stag with it, going shshsh-shshsh like an ostler. The preposterous old satyr, purple as he bent to polish the antler, winking at Julia through the tangle of tines, made the warehouseman nervous and talkative. 'A very fine 'ed and worth every penny of two, twelve, six which I couldn't take a penny less – the horn alone is worth twice the sum named for the manufacture of fancy goods - penknife handles, sir, carving forks. And when ground is used for the cure of certain female ailments as no doubt your good lady knows, sir: I am a married man myself, ahem. Oh sir, you may say "Oh, it is a very old article." Why, yes, sir, it *is* an old article and who denies it? But a horned stag is a very old article by nature. In its nature, sir, a stag is an old article.'

'Yes, yes,' said Edwin to the telephone, looking dutiful and attentive into the distemper three inches from his nose. 'Yes, Lady Dogge. Yes: yes. I'm very sorry, Lady Dogge; but it's finished now, Lady Dogge. Oh, please don't say that, Lady Dogge. No, Lady Dogge. Yes, Lady Dogge. Good-bye, Lady Dogge.'

'The bitch,' he said, but not very loud. He sat down quickly to his desk and read through the manuscript. 'It will do,' he said, without conviction, and crammed it into an envelope.

He hurried down the shallow flights of stairs, iron-bound cement in a chocolate-painted well that clanged and echoed, down to the wan hall with its lavatory tiles. The porter came out of his booth and watched him down the last four flights.

'Good afternoon,' he said to the porter, as he put the envelope into the slit. 'Is there any post?'

'Where's Mrs?' said the porter, staring up the stairs.

'She's away at the moment.'

'Oh. Visiting, isn't it?'

The porter was also the deputy hangman for the south-east region and the tenants had to humour his independence.

'Yes,' said Edwin. 'Has the postman been?'

'No,' he replied, putting his hand over his coat-pocket. 'No, I don't think. But there is a parcel for you. Mrs is leaving it this morning.'

'Then why did you ask where she was?'

'Oh I did not, Mr; and it is a big old parcel,' said the porter, suddenly changing his tone to one of close affection and laying his hand on Edwin's sleeve as if to test the quality of the cloth, 'I can have the string, isn't it?'

The porter had already unwrapped the greater part of the stag, and Edwin finished the unpacking there in the booth: then grasping the polished shield upon which the head was mounted he began his upward journey. At the third flight he had to change his hold, for the shield was too slippery and the head too heavy in front; but taking the creature round the neck he balanced the weight better, and although it was momentarily disagreeable to put his face against the old rough hairiness he soon grew accustomed to it and after a flight or two he did not mind at all. They went up, cheek by jowl, very well balanced, and with the same noble antlers shading them like an open-work umbrella; and as he climbed – far happier than when he had gone down – Edwin reflected upon this token of his wife's esteem, this mute forerunner of her prompt return.

'I had almost begun to think – ' he confided to the stag. And 'It will be very useful,' he said to himself as he opened the door, 'and although it is far too large and spreading for the lobby, I will fix it solidly to my bedroom wall after I have done the washing-up, and I will hang my clothes on it at night.'

Samphire

---◦◦◦---

SHEER, SHEER, the white cliff rising, straight up from the sea, so high that the riding waves were nothing but ripples on a huge calm. Up there, unless you leaned over, you did not see them break, but for all the distance the thunder of the water came loud. The wind, too, tearing in from the sea, rushing from a clear, high sky, brought the salt tang of the spray on to their lips.

They were two, standing up there on the very edge of the cliff: they had left the levelled path and come down to the break itself and the man was crouched, leaning over as far as he dared.

'It *is* a clump of samphire, Molly,' he said; then louder, half turning, 'Molly, it *is* samphire. I *said* it was samphire, didn't I?' He had a high, rather unmasculine voice, and he emphasized his words.

His wife did not reply, although she had heard him the first time. The round of her chin was trembling like a child's before it cries: there was something in her throat so strong that she could not have spoken if it had been for her life.

She stepped a little closer, feeling cautiously for a firm foothold, and she was right on him and she caught the smell of his hairy tweed jacket. He straightened so suddenly that he brushed against her. 'Take care,' he cried, 'I almost trod on you. Yes, it *was* samphire. I said so as soon as I saw it from down there. Have a look.'

She could not answer, so she knelt and crawled to the edge. Heights terrified her, always had. She could not close her eyes; that only made it worse. She stared unseeing, while the brilliant air and the sea and the noise of the sea

45

assaulted her terrified mind and she clung insanely to the thin grass. Three times he pointed it out, and the third time she heard him so as to be able to understand his words. '. . . fleshy leaves. You see the fleshy leaves? They used them for pickles. Samphire pickles!' He laughed, excited by the wind, and put his hand on her shoulder. Even then she writhed away, covering it by getting up and returning to the path.

He followed her. 'You noted the *fleshy leaves*, didn't you, Molly? They allow the plant to store its nourishment. Like a cactus. Our *native* cactus. I *said* it was samphire at once, didn't I, although I have never actually seen it before. We could almost get it with a stick.'

He was pleased with her for having looked over, and said that she was coming along very well: she remembered – didn't she? – how he had had to persuade her and persuade her to come up even the smallest cliffs at first, how he had even to be a little firm. And now there she was going up the highest of them all, as bold as brass; and it was quite a dangerous cliff too, he said, with a keen glance out to sea, jutting his chin; but there she was as bold as brass looking over the top of it. He had been quite right insisting, hadn't he? It was worth it when you were there, wasn't it? Between these questions he waited for a reply, a 'yes' or a hum of agreement. If he had not insisted she would always have stayed down there on the beach, wouldn't she? Like a lazy puss. He said, wagging his finger to show that he was not quite in earnest, that she should always listen to her Lacey (this was a pet name that he had coined for himself). Lacey was her lord and master, wasn't he? Love, honour and obey?

He put his arm round her when they came to a sheltered turn of the path and began to fondle her, whispering in his secret night-voice, Tss-tss-tss, but he dropped her at once when some coast guards appeared.

As they passed he said, 'Good-day, men,' and wanted to

stop to ask them what they were doing but they walked quickly on.

In the morning she said she would like to see the samphire again. He was very pleased and told the hotel-keeper that she was becoming quite the little botanist. He had already told him and the nice couple from Letchworth (they were called Jones and had a greedy daughter: he was an influential solicitor, and Molly would be a clever girl to be nice to them), he had already told them about the samphire, and he had said how he had recognized it at once from lower down, where the path turned, although he had only seen specimens in a hortus siccus and illustrations in books.

On the way he stopped at the tobacconist on the promenade to buy a stick. He was in high spirits. He told the man at once that he did not smoke, and made a joke about the shop being a house of ill-*fume*; but the tobacconist did not understand. He looked at the sticks that were in the shop but he did not find one for his money and they went out. At the next tobacconist, by the pier, he made the same joke to the man there. She stood near the door, not looking at anything. In the end he paid the marked price for an ash walking stick with a crook, though at first he had proposed a shilling less: he told the man that they were not ordinary summer people, because they were going to have a villa there.

Walking along past the pier towards the cliff path, he put the stick on his shoulder with a comical gesture, and when they came to the car park where a great many people were coming down to the beach with picnics and pneumatic rubber toys he sang, *We are the boys that nothing can tire: we are the boys that gather samphire*. When a man who was staying in the same hotel passed near them, he called out that they were going to see if they could get a bunch of jolly good samphire that they had seen on the cliff yesterday. The man nodded.

It was a long way to the highest cliff, and he fell silent for a little while. When they began to climb he said that he would never go out without a stick again; it was a fine, honest thing, an ashplant, and a great help. Didn't she think it was a great help? Had she noticed how he had chosen the best one in the shop, and really it was very cheap; though perhaps they had better go without tea tomorrow to make it up. She remembered, didn't she, what they had agreed after their discussion about an exact allowance for every day? He was walking a few feet ahead of her, so that each time he had to turn his head for her answer.

On the top it was blowing harder than the day before, and for the last hundred yards he kept silent, or at least she did not hear him say anything.

At the turn of the path he cried, 'It is still there. Oh jolly good. It is still there, Molly,' and he pointed out how he had first seen the samphire, and repeated, shouting over the wind, that he had been sure of it at once.

For a moment she looked at him curiously while he stared over and up where the plant grew on the face of the cliff, the wind ruffling the thin, fluffy hair that covered his baldness, and a keen expression on his face; and for a moment she wondered whether it was perhaps possible that he saw beauty there. But the moment was past and the voice took up again its unceasing dumb cry: Go on, oh, go on, for Christ's sake go on, go on, go on, oh go *on*.

They were there. He had made her look over. 'Note the fleshy leaves,' he had said; and he had said something about samphire pickle! and how the people at the hotel would stare when they brought it back. That was just before he began to crouch over, turned from her so that his voice was lost.

He was leaning right over. It was quite true when he said that he had no fear of heights: once he had astonished the workmen on the steeple of her uncle's church by walking among the scaffolding and planks with all the aplomb of a steeplejack. He was reaching down with his left arm, his right leg doubled under him and his right arm extended on the grass: his other leg was stretched out along the break of the cliff.

Once again there was the strong grip in her throat; her stomach was rigid and she could not keep her lip from trembling. She could hardly see, but as he began to get up her eyes focused. She was already there, close on him – she had never gone back to the path this time. God give me strength: but as she pushed him she felt her arms weak like jelly.

Instantly his face turned; absurd, baby-face surprise and a shout unworded. The extreme of horror on it, too. He had been half up when she thrust at him, with his knee off the ground, the stick hand over and the other clear of the grass. He rose, swaying out. For a second the wind bore up his body and the stick scrabbled furiously for a purchase on the cliff. There where the samphire grew, a little above, it found a hard ledge, gripped. Motionless in equilibrium for one timeless space – a cinema stopped in action – then his right hand gripped the soil, tore, tore the grass and he was up, from the edge, crouched, gasping huge sobbing draughts of air on the path.

He was screaming at her in an agonized falsetto interrupted by painful gasps, searching for air and life. 'You *pushed* me, Molly you – *pushed* me. You – *pushed* me.'

She stood silent, looking down and the voice rushed over her. You *pushed* – you *pushed* me – Molly. She found she could swallow again, and the hammering in her throat was less. By now his voice had dropped an octave: he had been speaking without a pause but for his gasping – the gasping had stopped now, and he was sitting there normally. '. . . not well; a spasm. Wasn't it, Molly?' he was saying; and she heard him say 'accident' sometimes.

Still she stood, stone-still and grey and later he was saying

'. . . *possibly* live together? How can we *possibly* look at one another? After this?' And sometime after it seemed to her that he had been saying something about their having taken their room for the month . . . accident was the word, and spasm, and not well – fainting? It was, wasn't it, Molly? There was an unheard note in his voice.

She turned and began to walk down the path. He followed at once. By her side he was, and his face turned to hers, peering into her face, closed face. His visage, his whole face, everything, had fallen to pieces: she looked at it momentarily – a very old terribly frightened comforting-itself small child. He had fallen off a cliff all right.

He touched her arm, still speaking, pleading. 'It *was* that, wasn't it, Molly? You didn't push me, Molly. It was an accident . . .'

She turned her dying face to the ground, and there were her feet marching on the path; one, the other; one, the other; down, down, down.

The Clockmender

SUDDENLY he was awake. His waking had the abrupt
completeness of an electric light, entirely off one second and
entirely on the next. This was no warm transition from a
confused doze to a partial consciousness of the world, an
awareness that would begin with the pillow, the position of
his relaxed body under the bedclothes, and that would
work slowly outwards to a comfortable realization of the
world, with himself in it, each piece falling naturally into
its accustomed place. No. This was an abrupt and full
awakening from a profound sleep; and the world that
presented itself was naked, instantly concrete, sharply
defined and entire.

He knew at once that there was no hope whatever of
drifting off again, and he realized with horror that the grey
light in the room could not have been there much above an
hour. He looked over the edge of his bed at the pair of
chronometers on the low table: on each severe dial the
steel hands showed five twenty-five. Some disturbance,
some chance noise had cheated him of three hours of sleep.

It was a tragedy. He would have to get up very soon,
for in a short time the insistent restlessness of his body
would make bed intolerable and he would be forced into
waste of another day, another cruelly lengthened day.

Three hours more to serve. It was a tragedy: and it was
so unfair. He had spun out the evening until well past ten
o'clock, and he had won the right to sleep until eight or
even nine. He had gone on polishing the new-cut pallets of
the Knibb clock until they were almost beyond perfection,
burnishing the faces with a slip of agate – four thousand

lengthways strokes to each of the four angles. Two hours and thirteen minutes, timing each stroke by the beat of a half-seconds pendulum. That had earned him his rest, surely.

But no. Here he was at half-past five, irrevocably awake and committed to the day. Something tapped on the window and scraped across the glass: that must have been it, he thought, looking round; the long thin branch from the wistaria: it should have been pruned years ago, when it was a stray twig; but now it had grown long enough to reach the windowpane as the cold wind of the dawn dragged it against the side of the house.

He had planted that wistaria himself when first he had the place. In those days he had been up with the first light – he had been up *before* the first light – for he had often switched on the lamp as he dressed. He had dressed in his gardening clothes at once, to lose no time.

He had dressed then: he had willingly gone through the process of putting on all those garments, selecting, buttoning, tying, turning right-side out, doing-up; every day he had accepted the series of motions that would have to be reversed at night. At that time he had been able to accept the drill of left arm – right arm, left leg – right leg, left foot – right foot, and its perpetual repetition. And the prospect of it had never kept him daunted in his bed: he remembered his eager getting up – springing up – in spite of his warm sleepiness, from a bed where he had gone to sleep still working out the details of the garden. Of the kitchen garden, mostly, for although he had a brave show of flowers it was the parallelograms of the kitchen garden that fascinated him – the drilled rows of the potatoes and the cabbages – and he would lie fighting against sleep while he carried out the mental arithmetic designed to show the total yield of his thirty-five rows of main-crop potatoes if each plant yielded an average of three and a quarter pounds.

He remembered that now, as a fact: but he could no longer comprehend the once-vital urgency that had made

it a fact; he could not feel that there was anything at all in
common between the young man who had so enthusiastically
worked out the cropping-plan for a seven-year rotation;
who had, as the winter days grew short, dug the last double
trenches by the light of a hurricane lamp to be doubly ready
for the longed-for spring. Nothing in common between the
man who had dug and cherished the garden and the one
who now had not even visited the lower plot, the head-high
jungle of nettles and fool's parsley, for months and months.
Yet there was a physical continuity: the body was the same.
And it was the same bed in which he lay. The wistaria, too,
was a speaking witness. He had planted it, a straggling
whipple, over the buried carcass of an ass, and now its trunk
was like a grey python on the wall and its untended branches
rapped against his bedroom windowpane.

One day, perhaps, he would go down through the tangle
of roses to the kitchen garden and see whether among the
rank growth below the apple-trees he could find the remains
of his hives. It would be interesting to know if any of the
colonies had survived. Once, nearly three years ago it must
be now, he had seen a swarm clustered like an uncoloured
shining bunch of grapes on the handle of a forgotten spade.
They might have been from his own bees.

He would go down. But at the thought of actually doing
it, of fixing a time for doing it, of dressing in order to do it,
so great a physical repulsion seized him that to escape he
turned his head further down into his pillow and fixed his
eyes on the glass window in the side of the chronometer case.

The cylindrical hairspring contracted, swelled, contracted, the pulsation of a metal heart: he could not see the
slow, even swing of the balance-wheel, but behind the links
of the fusee, taut between the helix and the drum, he caught
the recurrent flash of the scape-wheel pinion: the soft gleam
of brass in the grey light was like the ever-returning wink
of a lighthouse, impersonal, utterly reliable, continuing an
indefinite series that drew out towards infinity; and in time

the beautiful monotony steadied his mind. Now he could think more evenly of the prospects of the lengthened day.

They were horrible. But they were not so horrible as thinking of the garden and of all those other things that had once filled his life. Some of them he had cut out deliberately: he had amputated them when each in turn had threatened to grow into an exclusive obsession. Seeing his friends, for example; and his exact system of economy – that had been one of the hardest, but he had succeeded in the end, and now his rows of account books, with every item of expenditure balanced against each incoming penny, had remained unopened these many years. It had been so delightful to calculate the market cost of the garden produce: the bees had had their ledger too: and it had been such a keen triumph to deny himself for the reward of carrying over a surplus from one month to the next. But now he spent as he chose, not even taking a note of it; and in the second drawer of his desk the dividend vouchers piled up, still uncounted; and somewhere there was a clip of uncashed cheques.

This amputation had been successful, but it had required a dreadful effort: other things had fallen away of themselves. He had deliberately shut his door to callers, but he had never of set purpose opposed himself to books or music. Yet the one was as successful as the other, and it would now mean as much forbidden and indeed impossible effort to open the piano and play as to open the door and engage in conversation with a casual visitor.

They had shredded away, all these things – all positive action, all doing, had retreated obediently to the other side of what was tolerable. When he got up now, he would slip on his dressing-gown. More than that would be – he wrenched away from the thought.

What do fleas do when they are not biting? he wondered. Or dogs, when they are not fighting, eating or being taken for a walk – house dogs? They must fall back into the stagnant pool of time. What a universal cruelty, repeated throughout an infinity of members, to be suspended in the fantastically deliberate flow of time, with no possible escape but the even greater horror of the farther limit, where there was no time at all. For very small creatures perhaps it would be worse: a day might be a year for them, by reason of their size.

Oh the days and the unending hours, he thought, turning his head from side to side. Yet all the time one's body lived eagerly in the flow: hair and nails – every night his unwanted beard thrust up another hundredth of an inch; and continuously, without a second's pause, his skin renewed itself, thrust on by innumerable subtle needless combinations of blind vitality.

Why should the clocks alone have stayed? There seemed to be no reason for their permanence, but in the next room, among the desert of unopened books, there was his workbench, clean, sharp-angled and precise with its rows of tools, broaches, dies and taps, throws, pliers of different shapes and sizes, all ranged so exactly that by now he could pick up each separate tool without taking his eyes from his work. This perfect arrangement called for years and years of use, but then of course he had begun years and years ago. To begin with the old grandfather in the hall could not be made to go: the watchmaker in the village was ill, so he had tinkered with it himself. A common thirty-hour movement, no more, but the simple mechanism, the wonderfully clear train of cause and effect, fascinated him and when he eventually mastered it, when the clock was ticking comfortably, he felt the strangest triumph. He bought books on clocks and even began to collect them in a small way: with the pleasure they brought him came the reproaches of his conscience – it was excessive and disproportionate to spend twelve hours a day for a week in wrestling inexpertly (he was inexpert then) with the escapement of a repeating verge – but in this case, and in this case alone, the reproach died of itself. The proposition that clocks should go was unanswerable. It was of absolute importance that they should go, should measure time exactly, and he concentrated all his powers to the task. He also bought more clocks.

'Well,' Dr Provis said, almost the last time he ever came to the house, 'I suppose it is a harmless way of killing time.' The remark was approving in substance but it was delivered with a kind of sneer: resenting this, he countered with a shrug of his shoulders and a half turn of his body. 'Ha, ha,' he replied. 'I think there is a difference, Provis, between *killing* time and *measuring* it.'

And then again, the full significance apart, this was an activity in which he could control all the factors: for clocks, rightly adjusted, would go; they had none of the intolerably frustrating imponderables of living things, yet for him they were alive enough. They exactly suited him; and his somewhat inhuman persistence suited them.

But in the last eighteen months the area of his pleasure had contracted. By now he had a very high degree of skill; he could cut a pair of pallets for any escapement the old clockmakers had ever made, and in case of need he could even produce a new scape wheel. But a new scape wheel was now a few hours' work: once it had been the toil of weeks, and once he had felt a tingling elation as the new wheel first revolved, ticked, and swung the doubtful pendulum. And by now he had an example of every variant; there was no new principle to be explored, and by the rules of his conscience he could not clutter up his house with clocks that would essentially be no more than duplicates of those he had already. Nor, now that he had the highest degree of manual ability, could he interfere with a clock that was going perfectly. Once, with no more than a half-imagined hint of irregularity, he had felt justified in stripping a clock and searching over every part of it, perfecting as he went; but he could not do so now. It must not be blind activity, doing for the sake of doing: it had to have the dignity of an end in view. That was a discipline which he must never, never break, or the whole thing would fall into an incoherent mockery.

He could do it all now, verge pallets, deadbeat pallets, ordinary anchor pallets . . . abruptly he remembered his evening's work. To make a long night's sleep more sure he had stayed up to finish the pallets of the small Knibb clock. He had finished the work entirely: he should have kept it for today. Without it the grey hours stretched away in an endless plain without anything at all to break the horrifying blank.

He lay there with the utter vacancy before him, and if no relief had come he might have screamed at last. But at a few minutes to six the arm lifted from the locking plate of the Graham bracket clock; the detent wheel spun three-quarters of a turn; the hoop wheel moved the distance of two pinion leaves; the clock was ready to strike six. It was immediately followed by the others. His practised ear heard the cocking of the clocks, and a springing hope made his thin heart beat.

There was no hope from the Knibb clock: that would be going accurately, with no shadow of a doubt. It was perfectly in beat and he had regulated its pendulum to the last hairs-breadth: he knew that clock. But it seemed to him that in his sleep he had heard the Tompion drop a stroke, as if the locking plate were worn: it had given trouble seven years before. Unless it were a dream it would be the Tompion, and it would probably have happened at three – he heard them through his sleep, he knew. And if that were so it would now strike five, not six. Five strokes instead of six: it would be an escape, a reprieve for one more day at least.

He listened intently, breathing shallow not to make a noise. The hands of the two chronometers crept in perfect unison towards the point of six. In the next room an assembly of long-case clocks, bracket clocks, wall clocks, and table clocks stood poised to bell out the time. Only the equation clocks and the big regulator would not say anything: they had no bells. The others, the converted Cromwellian lantern clock, the early Fromanteel, the Tompion, the Graham deadbeat, the Mudge, the Quare, the Harrison, had all raised their striking trains. They stood there in no order, here and there about the book-lined room: he cared nothing for the beauty of their cases and some rested on rough trial benches, stripped of their hoods and covered from the dust with glass bell jars. Their ticking filled the room with a strange, depressingly urgent confusion of sound as they flicked the present by. Brass and iron insects, horrifying in their nakedness and numbers, perpetually eating time.

He waited, and as the moment drew nearer and nearer he clenched his fists under the bedclothes.

The first clock dropped and whirred; the pin gathered the tail of the hammer and bore down upon it. The first stroke rang out pure, but the second was lost in the clangour of the other clocks, whirring, striking faster or slower, all bawling out that it was six, pinning the moment down.

Straining his head up from his pillow he followed the deep, smooth tone of the Tompion through the competing din. At the fourth stroke his expression changed, and at the fifth his face lost its humanity. Now there was the racing pause between the fifth stroke of that one bell and the sound of the sixth, if it should ever come. The pause lengthened at last beyond the possibility of another stroke – it had missed for sure; but until the last of the clocks had finished, the Graham with its melancholy toll, his face did not change. Only then, when the last sound had died to a humming in the bell, did he allow his strained-up head to move. It sank down, and his eyelids fluttered over his eyes; but in another minute he was up, his fingers twitching with activity. He threw the dressing-gown over his shoulders and shuffled quickly to the door: and as he opened it he lowered his head to conceal the pale smile on his face.

The Chian Wine

———◆◦◆———

WHEN first he came to Saint-Felíu the middle and indeed the dark ages still hung about the streets, while the beach was classical antiquity itself. The village was so heavily fortified, with two castles, five towers and a massive surrounding wall – so heavily fortified against the Spaniards, the Algerine corsairs and the inhuman people from the neighbouring province that there was little room for the three thousand inhabitants. In the course of centuries they had crammed their houses into narrow winding lanes, so close that their roofs, viewed from the nearby hills, resembled a swarm of bees, with never an open place to be seen.

Hanging from his window over one of these deep lanes in the hope of air – he had been ordered to the Mediterranean for the air – Alphard saw a world he had imagined long past and gone: in those days mules paced by; women with loads poised on their heads – heads that turned slowly, with infinite grace, to watch the town-crier as he beat his drum and announced death or the arrival of goat-cheese in the market-place. Tumblers appeared, a family of dumb acrobats; they spread a dusty mat on the cobbles and tumbled there in the street, turning somersaults and contorting their lithe dusty bodies until it seemed they must come apart, while their dumb, thin-faced children looked up with open hands to the windows, catching the sparse shower of little coins: and at All Hallows a Basque brought his dancing bear – they slept together, by arrangement, in the cellar of Alphard's house. The life of the village went on in the street. At noon the men lit fires of vine-cuttings outside their doors, and the smell of grilling fish wafted up;

59

family quarrels also came out into the open, and once he saw a stone-faced woman bring a chair and sit outside a door all day and half the night until her husband should come out. Every morning the women carried pots of filth mixed with ashes to the edge of the sea; every morning they and their daughters went to the pump recessed into the opposite house for water; every evening the grandmothers came back from the hills loaded with an immense faggot, held by a band across their foreheads. Every evening the ass that belonged to Alphard's landlord picked its way through the people, through the innumerable dogs and cats, and walked up the ladder-like stairs, followed some minutes later by its master, a man with a fair-sized vineyard and a market-garden, and one of the few who did not go out with the fishing-boats. The fishermen all had vineyards too in the terraced hills behind; and as peasants they lived by the rhythm of the sun for half the year, rising before dawn and sleeping in the heat of the day; in the due seasons they worked, sprayed, sulphured and pruned their vines, and every autumn, when the grapes came home in narrow carts or in eared tubs slung to the saddles of hump-backed mules – brass-studded, old crimson saddles – the streets ran purple and the smell of fermenting wine hung over the town. But as fishermen they lived by the moon, rising according to its motions and gathering in the darkness at the gate that gave on to the open strand. Sometimes they came back at moonset, sometimes not until the bell was ringing for high mass, but more usually at dawn; and when, as it often happened, the cock upstairs made sleep impossible, Alphard would go down to watch them.

It was here on the beach that the ancient world showed purest: with his back to the town he could forget the two or three thousand intervening years. The sea was timeless, of course; and apart from the baroque church on his left the shore-line too was quite unchanged. The long, brilliantly-painted, high-prowed boats with pagan symbols on their bows might have been launched for the siege of Troy: the men who sailed them, rounding the jetty under their archaic lateen sails or sweeping in when the breeze failed them, might have been bringing back the Golden Fleece. In fact they usually brought anchovies; and when the catch was heavy they would heave to there at the edge of the sea, picking the silver fish out of their nets, tossing them into baskets. They would then carry the baskets up the beach – a line of men in red Phrygian caps and washed-blue drawers staggering abreast through the shingle with these gleaming fish between them, while their house-cats came running out, tails erect, each to its own basket. One day, when he was watching, a fisherman handed him a small amphora: after the south-east gales they often came up in the nets, tearing the delicate mesh, and usually the men broke them on the gunwale to make sure they would sink for good; but this was a neat little jar; it had done no harm; and Joseph thought Monsieur Alphard might like to have it, the seal being still intact.

It was indeed: beneath the incrustations of the sea the wax stated that Aristolochus of Chios had made this wine; and beneath the seal the wine, or at least a liquid of some sort, could be heard and felt. 'I shall try it some day,' said Alphard, setting it on a tripod from the hearth. 'Wine of the nth Olympiad! I shall try it one day, when I have good news.'

Now ten and twenty years had passed, a generation and more, and the wine still stood among the books, its seal unbroken. Alphard himself looked much the same, though his hair was greyer still, his sight was dim, his taste for music and for reading had almost gone, and even his longing for salvation; and his long solitary walks had shrunk to an occasional stroll along the jetty: his heart was quite shrivelled with habitual woe and its consequent selfishness; but he still cared for his everlasting bird and for the mice that came for its seed. He still looked with automatic eagerness for a letter in the morning, although by now he would not have known what to do with it if it had come; he still divided his morning, after early mass and the post, between *Le Monde* and the *Gazette de Lausanne*, lunched at home with his bird on a piece of cheese, dined at the Café du Commerce, and then sat for an hour or two over his coffee on the terrace, watching the passers-by and the sea beyond. He had become inured to the tragedy of growing old; his jets of rebellion had faded, and he knew that presently he too must die – he could hear the crier's voice announcing it before the goat's cheese and the eels. Yet still for the children of the village Monsieur Alphard in his dark and shabby suit was as unchanging and as little noticed as the clock-tower.

But Saint-Felíu had changed, changed almost out of recognition. Pert white houses had sprung up outside the walls, with red-brick well-heads over nothing, gnomes, plastic storks; drains carried the filth into the viscid sea, now spoilt at last; water ran in every house; bottled gas or electricity had replaced the faggot-bearers; the braying of the conch was no longer heard, announcing a haul of mackerel, to be given to anyone who chose to bring a dish; what was left of the fishing-fleet ran on diesel-oil, distributed by a scarlet pump in the sea-gate itself; and the well-clothed younger generation no longer spoke the ancient tongue. At the autumn fair of the patron saint raucous microphones had replaced the human voice; the bear, the magpie that picked your fortune from the cards, the sword-swallower, the performing fleas, the fire-eater, were no longer to be seen, nor the pig-faced woman; and the hand-cranked roundabout had given way to an enormous whirling mass of supersonic planes. Hotels abounded – the Café du Commerce was now the fifty-roomed Commanderie du Soleil – and in high summer the villagers wandered like strangers among the tourist hordes: out of an obscure sense of shame the men had laid aside their red caps and broad sashes and the women their white lace coiffes. The ass and the poultry had long since vanished from Alphard's house. After a marriage the sheets no longer hung from the window: no ribald voice called up 'How much for a pint of pigeon's blood?'

'Yet still,' he said to Halévy as they sat there after dinner, 'the spirit of the place is quite unaltered. This is not the Spanish coast, whose soul has gone, quite gone. Whatever you may say, these people have kept their integrity: this is a true, an eternal microcosm . . .'

'When I used to come here as a boy,' said Halévy, 'Louise made the best fish soup known to man – pounded lobster-claws, a sea-devil's liver, the garlicked bread singing from the pan. Now she has hired a fellow with a tall white cap, and the soup comes out of a packet: I detected the criminal industrial crumbs, uncooked, this very evening. And this is not even the tourist-season. There is no excuse. No: it breaks my heart to contradict you, but these people have lost their sense of beauty. The doctored wine alone, and what they buy from me, must convince you of that. Here too the past has died: two thousand years of tradition have died! There is no bridge between the jet-age and the past.'

'Monsieur le Curé,' cried Alphard, rising from his chair and bowing to the cassocked priest, 'good evening to you. There,' he said to Halévy, 'there is your bridge – one of your bridges. The Church has not changed.'

Halévy smiled, raising his shoulders and spreading his hands; but he only said, 'He seems an excellent man, to be sure; it does me good to see him.'

Alphard felt the strength of Halévy's tactfulness and the naivety of his own remark in the present circumstances, and he cried, 'Not changed essentially, not here, I mean. The vernacular is so close to Latin any way that it makes little difference. The natural piety of the village is the same as it always was. Take my grocer Fifine, for example: she has sugar blessed on Saint Blaise's day, and whenever you have a sore throat she gives you half a dozen lumps – *gives* them, I say. Because to sell a blessed object would be gross impiety. There is your true mediaeval spirit, vigorously alive in the midst of electric refrigerators. Or take our curious vespers this day week, in which they have used the vernacular ever since the night of time.' He paused, recollecting that the traditional proceedings at Saint-Felíu on Good Friday were far too truly mediaeval to describe to Halévy. He was an Avignon Jew who had recently opened a small gallery outside the sea-gate, not far from the church, where he exhibited a few young painters and bought antiques for his brother's shop in Paris. He was old and fat and he had a mane of white hair; he meant to retire to Saint-Felíu, with the gallery for fun. Hitherto he had known the village only in the summer.

'What is so curious about your vespers?' he asked.

'Or take our bull-fight at Assumption,' said Alphard, feigning not to hear. 'There is continuity for you . . . and apart from anything else, these people are still at the mercy of the sea for one half of their living and of the sun for the other half: they dare not presume, or go whoring after other gods. They must keep the ancient ways, so long as the ancient ways keep them. But speaking of continuity, I should like to show you my jar of Chian wine one day. The seal is unbroken – a seal pressed at least two thousand years ago! We might even try it.'

Halévy did not follow the sequence of these observations – how could he? – but he saw that Alphard wished to change the subject, and he said that he should be very happy to see and even, if he were allowed, to try the Chian wine. 'I shall be back before Easter, to get the place ready for the tourists. First I have to go to Gosol, where a man tells me his cousin has a Romanesque Virgin he might sell. I doubt the story very much. A true twelfth-century Virgin is scarcely to be hoped for today – all that were portable have already been sold. But I shall go: I love those strong, pitiless faces, even when they are fakes.'

Good Friday's dawn could not be seen for the clouds coming

up from the south: a hot brooding day with a great many flies about. They even came into the cool depths of the church where Alphard was listening to a foolish young Dominican rattling away – an involved, enthusiastic sermon about ecumenism. The friar was in favour of it, but that was all his hearers could make out, since the reasoning was tenuous in the first place and the preacher had lost even that thread early on. The greater part of the congregation sat quietly as the excited, electrically-amplified voice went on and on, booming from loudspeakers hung in the aisles. The acoustics were poor, but even if the Dominican had been content with the voice God gave him most of the older women would not have understood his French. They stared before them in a mild, holy stupor, watching the candles flicker or the choirboys scratching themselves as they read their comics: they did not seem to mind the flies, either. Alphard wondered at their patience. He himself had out-lived his desires or had seen them dwindle into mere velleities – nothing mattered very much – but he had not outlived testiness, and as he brushed away a cluster of heavy, sluggish flies he muttered 'frying in Hell . . . frying in Hell.' He had had the greatest respect and affection for John XXIII as a man, but as a pope he thought him utterly disastrous – the results of his actions were utterly disastrous. Temerity, wild zeal, enthusiasm . . . Could it really be true that he was a freemason, a Communist?

The tedious friar came down from the pulpit at last, but he contrived to give the mass a new-fangled twist at the very end: if Alphard understood him right he asked for the congregation's blessing.

'At least one will know what to expect this afternoon,' he said indignantly, dipping his hand into the dried-up stoup. 'That will be a comfort.' Their old priest would be taking the traditional vespers, as he always did: a dear man, untouched by modernism – nothing histrionic there – no innovations to be feared. The moment he passed the door heat enveloped him completely; it was as though he had walked into a physical substance, for now the sirocco had set in. The flies were thicker still, hatching in multitudes from some hidden filth; and looking up to the ominous sky he saw that the mountains behind the town had that particular livid glow that often came before a storm.

'I hope it will not spoil the children's day,' he said. Not that he liked children: and most of the present crop, born since the village had grown so much richer from the tourists, were rough, aggressive, ill-mannered. They despised their illiterate parents; and their worshipping illiterate parents gave them far too much money. Far too much to the adolescent boys especially, who shrieked about the village streets on mopeds. Not that the girls were much better: a bold, gum-chewing, confident set. It seemed an unhappy generation for all its wealth; old and hard so very young. But still he hoped their day would not be spoiled. It was a particular ceremony, essentially for them; and it linked them with a very distant past – to the Crusades, in all probability. Many of them were dressed up for it already. He saw Fifine, leading her niece and her hulking great nephew by the hand. The children (if the hairy Albert could be called a child) walked stiffly, their arms away from their fine new clothes, and the free hand of each held an enormous rattle, of the kind that whirls about its stem. Both looked over-excited, and there was a glow of anticipation on their aunt's Visigothic face as she steered them through the throng.

A few yards farther on the shutters of the gallery were up, but to his surprise Alphard saw Halévy in the door, sweeping vigorously. He was bare to the waist and sweat ran through the grizzled mat on his bosom: he was wearing a beaded skull-cap, however, presumably against the dust. Averting his eyes from the mat, Alphard said, 'Are you back already?'

Halévy said that in fact he was – that he had found no

Madonna – four hundred miles in pursuit of a myth – and that he was profoundly discouraged.

'Come and try my Chian wine this evening,' said Alphard. 'Come at half past six.'

'I should be very happy,' said Halévy. 'Thank you. Such a privilege.' They talked about the weather – Halévy said the mountains made him think of El Greco – and while they were talking a horseplaying band of youths and boys, throwing sand and stones at one another, lurched into them. 'Jean-Paul, what are you about? Dédé, say you are sorry to the gentleman,' cried Alphard.

No apology, no reply: only a 'tough guy' look.

'Ill-mannered brutes,' he said. 'Really, I am ashamed for the village. I beg your pardon.'

'They all seem over-excited today,' said Halévy. 'All the children. What are those rattles they are carrying, and why the saucepans?' But before Alphard could reply, he went on, 'Oh, I have a horrible piece of news for you. The municipality has forbidden sardines to be grilled in the street: it seems the tourists do not like the smell.'

'They may forbid until they grow black in the face,' cried Alphard, flushing. 'The past will have its rights. The past will rise up and have its rights.'

Alphard was not used to receiving guests, and after his lunch and his siesta he spent a considerable time setting his room in order, brushing the table, cleaning two glasses, moving chairs, angering the bird. Outside it was even hotter, dustier, and more oppressive. He was late for vespers and he slipped into a side-chapel: the ceremony was perfectly familiar to him now, although it had seemed so strange twenty years ago, and he 'found his place' as it were, without hesitation. The remaining psalms and antiphons followed their universal course and then the ancient local variation began, in the vernacular – the Magnificat and its antiphon, followed by the curé's address. Alphard understood the language pretty well, and as the address never varied year by year he followed it with ease: yet it was not really a very interesting address, except on historical grounds, being an allegory showing the relationship between the Church and the unbelievers under the outward likeness of the conduct of the lion towards the ass, taken straight from a mediaeval bestiary; and as the curé's triple r's and explosive participles rolled round the church Alphard's attention wandered. Sometimes his eyes strayed over the shrouded form of Saint Eulalie, following the ecstatic baroque swirl beneath the sheet; sometimes he looked at the instruments of the Passion, the lance, the sponge, the cruel pincers, hanging unveiled beyond the saint; and sometimes he gazed at the packed congregation. On most days their conduct left a great deal to be desired; awe and even common respect were wanting, and the people, above all the children, usually whispered, giggled and stared about. But now, in spite of the heat, the flies, their new clothes, and the temptation of their rattles, whistles, saucepans and drums, they were exemplary; every year they delighted in the piece about the lion, and this year their interest was even greater. Leaning forward in their seats they listened with the keenest attention to the unvarying description of the beast: 'His head is the head of a king and he has a terrible neck and a mane and his chest is vast and square: he holds his great tail high above the ground. His flattened legs come down to his huge feet, which are divided, with long hooked claws . . . the ass alone resists him, braying there in the wilderness.'

The curé never used the microphone, and his fine deep voice filled the church, each word as distinct as a stone. The description was done and now the allegory was to be unfolded and made plain: here he might well have lost his grasp upon his hearers as he went on, right through the list; but they knew the climax was coming, and they never stirred. '. . . and the tail of the lion is justice, divine justice high over us. The lion's leg is flattened, and here we see the coming of the Passion: the shape of his foot is God's own sign that the world is to be held by the clenched fist. The sharp crooked claws are vengeance against the Jews; and the ass, who is the evil ass but the Jews? With the terrible face of a lion He will appear to the Jews when He judges them, for they damned themselves . . .'

Now the tension was growing to its height. Alphard had heard this twenty times and more, but he too leaned forward on his chair.

'For they damned themselves: the Jews betrayed their king.' In the momentary pause all the children drew in their breath: every mouth was open, every tongue shaped to form the sound of D; and the moment the priest cried 'Death to the Jews!' they all burst out 'Death to the Jews!' an enormous shrilling, instantly drowned by the even greater din of rattles, whistles, saucepans, drums as they rushed in a body from the church, leaving the adults to listen to the collect, read in a mild and unemphatic routine voice.

To recover from the shattering din and to avoid the racing bands of children as they howled and whistled in the streets, blind with excitement, Alphard usually walked on the jetty for half an hour; but today he went straight back along the beach towards his house. The sirocco had dropped: a brooding calm.

There was indeed something unusual about the general hubbub: less of the high small-child piping and more of the crack-voiced adolescent bawl, with here and there a woman's shriek and the bass roaring of a man. But Alphard's mind was far away until he reached the diesel-pump. Here there was a dense crowd, an impenetrable swarm – every youth and child in Saint-Felíu – and something was terribly amiss. The fun had turned oh so sour: the smell of a bull-fight or worse. In the heat and the dust and the shouting he tried to push through: somewhere in the middle of that tight mob outside Halévy's gallery there was a rhythmic crash; and striving, thrusting his way through the smaller children on

69

the fringe he saw half a dozen great boys swinging a baulk of wood, a launching stretcher from the beach, swinging it end-on against the door - a battering-ram. All round the edge there were women screaming, grasping at their own children: astonished men and dogs came running. Alphard shouted 'Jean-Baptiste, Jojo, put it down – stop, stop at once,' but as he tottered there, children underfoot, children pulling at his legs, the door gave way and there was Halévy, terribly pale, his white hair streaming, with an antique, bell-mouthed gun in his hands. A high triumphant roar, the shriek of rattles, a shower of stones, and he fired. Alphard went down. Had he been hit? No. But the swarm of children struggling over him three-deep kept him in the dust and by the time he struggled to his feet it had happened. The jet of diesel-oil played straight into the shop: Alphard stood there, bumped into, unsteady, tossed from side to side, amazed, tears running down his face, shouting 'Stop, stop, stop,' and the flames shot up, straight into the windless air, mounting high, high under the black and swirling smoke, an enormous fire.

The men were there, hitting, kicking, turning off the pump. Alphard turned away and he came face to face with a small beaming round-faced child who had not yet understood the change, a child that danced still, marvelling at the fire, waving her rattle and chanting 'Death, death to the Jews.'

The Virtuous Peleg

———◆◇◆———

EVERY YEAR a great concourse of people come to the place
they call Kevin's tomb in the mountains and they pray him
to intercede for them, for although he is not a saint upon
the calendar – he is not that Kevin, but another – he is much
revered in those parts which is no doubt a great solace to
him as he burns for ever in the extreme torment aggravated
as it is by every device and artifice known to the fiend of hell.
The pilgrims suppose him to be well placed to intercede for
them, in which they are right, by far the most of them being
false lechers, damned in every inch.

Kevin was a young man when he first lived in the beehive
cells that stand around Deara. He had no inclination to the
warfare which was the occupation of his sept, nor to work,
and equally none to women; he was as soft as a cat and sober
in his discourse and he slept inordinately, which made him
fat despite the diet of Deara. In the first years of his life with
the holy monks he was unable to avoid a small share of the
work, but when his young cousin Peleg was allowed to join
him this was no longer the case, which was a consolation to
Kevin.

Peleg had little enough inclination in his nature to work,
but he revered his cousin, who had an awful and persuasive
way, and had been held up to Peleg as a man perfect all the
days of his life, and daily young Peleg forced his nature and
conquered this aversion and cleaned the cell and tilled the
apron of garden and carried stones from the common field.
The carrying of them, even the huge square ones, was easy
enough for Peleg, being the length and breadth of an ox as
he was, and that of the larger kind.

They did not hold Peleg in much estimation at Deara, for he had no learning and if they had known he was incapable of his letters even, Peleg would have been put out of the beehive cells and they would have made him go back to watching his father's herd of swine, a meagre herd that was watched already by his nine brothers.

Peleg was humble in his mind and freely acknowledged his deficiencies; he studied meekness and told over his letters by day and by night, but they ran by like water or the mist and he had no hold upon them, which made him low in his spirits: his mind would also turn of itself to young women, especially to the three daughters of Turlough who were so kind and loving to him; and whenever his mind did this he would leap up and plunge into the deep pool to his neck and tell over his letters. Kevin told him each time how wicked he was, and the monks would offer to scourge him at any time, by day or by night, whenever he felt himself invaded by the flesh or the Devil.

It was at about this time that news came to Deara of Brothen's wonderful voyage to the Picts, how he went on a millstone that happened to be on the shore, and he sleeping most of the way and without oar, rudder or sail, and how he had baptized seven Pictish kings in one day, eleven dukes with their families, with many other nobles and four large fields of ordinary people.

The news edified the monks of Deara, as well it might; but it seemed to Peleg that he noted a certain restraint, almost a sourness like that you may see on the face of the second man when he says how well the first has run. Peleg too felt that the honour of Deara was in some way lowered by this success from the north, and daily after he had returned thanks for the spread of the faith he prayed that some one of the holy men of Deara might be moved to take to the sea, to be wafted by ghostly hands to the pagan coast, there to meet a bloody martyrdom with unflinching delight or to convert fourteen kings with the numerous family of each while the sun should stand in admiration and the day grow long enough for the numbers of the common to pass the end of counting. He prayed especially that the reverend Kevin might be the chosen vessel: he prayed with fervour and his four bones were flayed and his blood soaked into the stone.

Days passed, and the monks of Deara looked at one another sideways and anxious, but none went near the strand.

Peleg watched Kevin for signs of a trance or an exaltation perhaps, but Kevin still moved slowly and slept the day long in his cell, waking to eat or to go through the motions of worship. The only hopeful sign at all was his increasing absent-mindedness; for day after day now he would forget that the stirabout was for two and he would eat it all, as well as the nuts.

Many days Peleg fasted and that apart from the usual fasts of Deara which were known in all the Christian world: it was for his soul's health, as he found one evening, it being Friday and his birthday. There was an angel sitting on the heap of stones by the side of the common field that Peleg was picking for ever.

'Now, Peleg,' said the angel. 'God and Mary to you.'

'God and Mary to you and Patrick, sir,' replied Peleg, with good manners all over his ugly face.

'I have two messages for you, Peleg,' said the angel, and he stuck a moment in his speech, and Peleg could see that the messages had flown out of his memory and it was a question whether he could get them back or no.

'I have two messages for you, Peleg,' he repeated, slowly and leaning upon the importance of his words.

'I am much obliged for your kindness, your reverence,' said Peleg. 'It must have been the weary road, the day being close and thunder coming.' It was a little at random that he was talking, to save the angel from embarrassment.

'Now I will tell you what it is, Peleg,' said the angel,

73

getting up off the heap of stones. 'Should you like to try a couple of falls with me? You was always the one for wrestling, I think.'

'If it would not be too forward in me, sir, I should welcome it of all things,' said Peleg. 'To try a couple of falls with your honour would give me all the pleasure in life.'

The angel stretched his arms and stamped his feet; he was a cheerful angel, the sort St Paul warned women about, and Peleg thought he had taken drink upon the way.

'I shall dust your jacket, mind,' said the angel, and he was right, for in five minutes he had put Peleg down on the flat of his back three times with a bang that made the dust fly up.

'Now sit down upon the stone, joy,' said the angel, 'for you are pale in the face, I see, and I will tell you the two messages. The first is, "Heaven helps those as help themselves," and the second is, "There are those who seem more than they appear to others or themselves notwithstanding the appearance of some as they would appear in the first place; or the contrary." '

Peleg thanked the angel many times over, and asked might he hear the blessed words again.

'Why, no, Peleg,' replied the angel slowly, getting himself ready to go. 'I doubt it would be exactly right for me to repeat them, being the way it is. But they will certainly echo again, and bear the most elegant fruit.'

So Peleg walked with the angel to the edge of the field, where the path came in, and said, 'If your reverence chooses to take the road, the path that crosses the bog by those willows is the best, and the second house on the way is Seamus's, where is the best refreshment and easy bedding, with butcher's meat every day of the week almost.'

'I know it,' said the angel. 'I was there on my way.' And he said as he went, 'Health and glory and salvation to you, Peleg,' and Peleg replied, 'A hundred thousand thanks to

you, your reverence, and glory and health and happiness
for ever to you.'

The messages did indeed re-echo in Peleg's mind, they
churned about until the inside of his head was full of night,
and there was no sense in it. He went wandering over the
bog in a daze until it was dark, and then he went vacantly
into his cell where Kevin was asleep, and lay down on the
hard floor.

He could not remember going to sleep, but he woke up
very suddenly in the dead hour of the night, his mind a
blaze of illumination: there was a little sickly moon but
enough to see by and he looked closely at Kevin who was in
the very depth of stupor and his mouth open. Peleg eased
up his chin gently to improve his appearance, and gently,
like a woman, gathered him up in his clothing as he lay
there and carried him out of the cell. As he had often done,
he struck the lintel with his bowed shoulders and bore off
a handsbreadth of skin, but the pain did not discommode
him nor the prodigious vast weight of his cousin and his
bulk overflowing.

The dew was thick on the grass and his footsteps showed
clear, running straight to the strand. There were boats
there, and three millstones of different sizes, but millstones
were for the beneficed clergy, abbots, bishops and deans, and
Peleg put Kevin into a little neat curach. The sleeping
Kevin groaned and settled himself and Peleg sat on a thwart
while the tide swept them out and away on the far, broad
ocean.

For hours and hours Peleg sat there in a holy calm, contemplating the beauty of the calm sea, for it was like a small
pond in its calmness and there was the long path of the
moon behind them. The air was warm and sweet like hay
to smell and the curach slipped through the quiet water,
creaking a little and the water making a little slipping noise
under it.

Dawn came up with the glory of heaven and still Kevin

slept. Peleg longed to wake him so that they could be speaking of the voyage; sometimes he moved with more noise than he needed, and sometimes he coughed, but it was not until just before tierce that Kevin moved. The fat man gaped stupidly at Peleg, with his mouth dragging open, and when Peleg bade him rejoice because they were on the sea moving fast with the push of unseen hands towards the heathen shore he made no reply. He stared wildly round the pale bowl of the sky, green and grey where it met the sea all round and no land, no land at all; unending waters stretching away and away to the edge of the world and the sun glittering on them. He moaned aloud as he sat there crouched, and Peleg told him of his angel and about the glory of their approaching mission. Kevin made no answer, but when Peleg said he thought they might sing a loud prayer, he leapt up and stood balancing in the curach as it rocked and screamed curses at Peleg with the worst words in the world so that Peleg wondered how he had ever come to know them: and Peleg grew weary of hearing Kevin staining his soul and he rocked the boat the way Kevin was not expecting it so he fell in over the edge and swam in the sea among the fishes of the deep, and monsters came into his mind as well as the fear of drowning. So Kevin was in a great taking and nearly dead from his various fears and the furious amount of salt water he had taken in while shouting under the sea and breathing there too, and he spoke civilly to his cousin Peleg to have him into the curach again, which Peleg did, though with difficulty.

Now Kevin lay in the bottom of the curach weeping with cold and so frightened that he had not the look of a white pudding, far less a man, and Peleg sat on the tail end of the boat thinking, while he trailed his hand in the water.

A little spirit came back into Kevin as the sun dried him and he asked had Peleg brought any food, but Peleg had not brought any food; then he said they ought to go back because he had no licence from his superior to be converting heathens and because there was a book in his cell of great power and efficacity and he did not know how he could turn them from their heathenish ways without its help, and if Peleg would turn back now he would get the book and the licence from his superior as well as some relics and they would start again in a more respectable vessel than a common curach stinking of old fish the way it did, and dangerous with its thin, leaky sides.

'There is no sail, reverend Kevin, nor oars, nor a rudder to turn with: furthermore, we are impelled by unseen hands.'

So Kevin lay down again in the bottom of the boat and groaned until the sun went down into the sea behind them and night spread over the waters and still the curach slipped on with the push of unseen hands.

In the morning the sun was in front of them again and at their side was a grey island rising high out of the sea: Peleg awoke from a kind sleep and there by the side of the curach was a seal watching for him to wake. He blessed the good seal, which was his custom, and the seal brought him a fish to his hand.

The island was full of sea-birds, white, black and pied, as full as a hive of bees, and their screaming awoke Kevin, who said they were fiends and cursed them. He wished to go on to the island to escape the sea and would have swum, for they passed very near, but he saw the seals as thick as a fair and he was afraid. 'They are fiends,' he said. 'The sea is full of fiends.'

The island sank into the sea behind them, but before it was quite down they saw land ahead stretching far to the either hand. Presently Peleg could discern the mouth of a broad river, and the curach went up into it, over the bar with no more than three inches of water covering it at this state of the tide, but that so godly quiet that they slipped over with no danger, and now Peleg saw on his left hand a sandy waste and on his right hand a rich, fruitful country, green and red where the soil showed.

Kevin's heart and courage had grown since they had crossed the bar, and he was talking when the curach grounded gently in the sand of the right-hand shore. The jar threw him flat on his face, so Peleg picked him out of the boat and put him on the dry sand, where he sank down in a heap, gasping. Peleg looked and he saw the neat curach turned about already and running easily through the water, which had waves now, though small. He watched it going on the broad waters and he felt a small quell in his heart, but only for a moment, he being maintained by the zeal of his mission.

They went up the shore, Kevin blaming Peleg very bitterly for letting the curach go, and into a green wood, where Peleg lit a fire, having returned thanks, and he cooked the fish, which was a mullet; and the heathen of those parts surrounded them in the bushes.

The first they knew of the heathen was a terrible howling and an ululating that would have daunted the heart of an emperor, it was so near and the men unseen. Then there was a shower of arrows and stones that tore the green leaves and the heathen rushed in upon them. They were painted orange and they carried long, bare knives and it was the way they had to flay all strangers on their coast. Peleg and Kevin without drawing breath for one peaceable word sprang, leapt and sped through the trees and beyond inland with all the agility in the world, running so fast they passed the startled deer, and the heathen ran after them to have their hides, but their heathenish cries and howling delayed them, whereas Peleg and Kevin ran without a word, seeing they needed their breath and could not be sparing it in hallooing and bawling aloud.

It was a wonder to see the fat man run with his face and belly quivering and shaking like the bag of a cow, but soon he faltered and cried out to Peleg, who took him by the hand and they raced over the strange country with flying strides and the heathen drawn out behind them, howling angrily in the distance, angrier as the distance grew.

For hours and hours they ran until they came to heathery land, high and rolling, with standing meres and bogs and they could see clear miles behind them with nobody following. It was a harsh and desolate country, and its brooks ran dark between black, steep banks. White mist curled in the lower parts and already with the coming of the night the mist was rising to cover the whole country.

On the top of a craggy piece they lay in a cave, a great deep cave that went back and back, and Peleg's mind troubled him because he had avoided his martyrdom and because he had uttered no peaceable or godly word to the heathen. Kevin wept from exhaustion and lasting terror and the pain of his feet as well as for the memory of the grey mullet uneaten by the woodland fire: he uttered a few watery prayers and slept in his moaning. But Peleg remained waking, working in his mind, and when the devils of the waste-land came they found him awake.

The sight of so many fiends at once appalled Peleg beyond the power of speech, and Kevin turned the colour of lead, with never a word in his mouth, though it opened and closed. The devils sat about the cave, quite easy, and lit it up with the effulgence of their persons.

The captain of the devils, a grand spotted one, spoke in a loud commanding voice to Peleg and said: 'Now, Peleg, we don't want but two words with you, just renounce the Trinity at once, if you please, and we'll cry quits.'

But Peleg said never a word, and he made no answer again when the captain of the devils said, 'It is only a form, you know; there is nothing to it, at all.' So the devil grew angry and sent for a rack and a portable furnace and when they had put down the rack, together with a variety of instruments like iron flails and saws which the messengers brought of their own motion, with a ringing clash on the floor and had set up the furnace the way the cave stank of brimstone the captain nodded to Peleg and said, 'We'll sort you directly, my man.' Then he turned sharp on Kevin and gave him the same order and he said, 'Kevin, stand up at once and renounce the Trinity out of hand,' and he stamped fire.

Kevin stood up at once, but Peleg cried to him to have courage. The devil nodded to a great hairy thing of uncertain shape that had been standing behind Peleg's neck all this time, breathing on him, and it struck him down and gagged him. He lay and heard Kevin renounce the Trinity and everything else he could lay his mind to, and indeed Kevin blasphemed until even the devils stretched their eyes and looked behind them.

'It's all very well,' said the oldest hob-devil to the Captain secretly behind his hand like a man at a fair, 'but we shan't have his soul for certain like this: he must be damned of his own will, you know.'

The Captain said, 'Sure, you're right, my dear, but if he's got a soul at all there would be hardly any taste in it, or flavour, as you might say. We'll not spend anything on getting it, so. However, try an ordinary temptation or two by all means, if you're so inclined.'

Then they turned to Peleg and threatened him like blackguards, but Peleg said, 'You old blackguards, the back of my hand to you all.'

Then they had him to the rack, but it was too small by half for one of his length, and even when they had it wound right up it hardly stretched him above an inch. So they started on him with their flails, but they had small confidence in them, seeing that Peleg's father had always beaten his sons whenever they did wrong with a holy rage far beyond the emulation of devils, and Peleg had often done wrong in his young days – nearly every day, indeed. When they were tired and had spoilt three of their flails they stopped and took Peleg into an inner cave. There they made him sleep and let him rest while they considered of what they should do. He woke up to find the three daughters of Turlough in the cave, they who had been so kind and loving to him before he went to Deara after holiness, and a voice said in his ear that he could have whichever he chose as a reward for his fortitude. But the devil himself could not have told the confusion in Peleg's heart at the sight of the three together, by reason of the passages he had had with each separately, and Peleg blushed fiery red and hid his face. The she-devils who personated the daughters of Turlough thought themselves scorned and they stepped out of the cave with bitter anger and said they had no business with geldings, nor with unnatural men, they said.

This put the devils out of countenance, for they saw they were improving Peleg's chance of salvation hour by hour, and this was poison and death to their minds. When they had tempted him with meat and drink and fire and water as well as with gold and silver and the promise of land with no success, they said he must be more holy than he looked, and the great scholar of the world, no doubt.

'There is only one way with these scholars,' said the Captain and he called for a pen. For seventy-three days they kept Peleg by while the Captain worked fourteen and fifteen hours a day and his claws grew long and curved for want of the wear of exercise and fiends ran hither and yon with sheets of paper at every hour on the heather of the waste-land. At the end the Captain had two books written, the one of elegant poems so lewd that they would have been a danger to St Anthony, and the other, in fine elm boards with silver clasps, a book of homilies so eloquent that they would have struck Chrysostom dumb, and they poisoned through and through with the creeping poison of a heresy so persuasive that no ecclesiastic much under the degree of a saint could have withstood it.

They put them by Peleg while he slept and they penned him up with them and a good, clear light and a reading desk and no other kind of diversion at all until his beard grew to the middle of his chest and they judged he had had time to damn himself. But Peleg had only opened the books once apiece to see were there capitals painted on gold with every variety of colour and beasts interlacing, but there were not, the Captain having no turn that way, and he had closed them without taking more thought, for his strength was not in reading and indeed he could not exactly recall above half a dozen of the letters themselves at this distance from Deara. He had spent his time in mortification and prayer and learning the meekness that he lacked, and particularly in praying for his cousin Kevin, which had done his own soul so much good that it was now practically white and in better shape than it had been since he was first capable of sin.

It was on a Friday that the Captain sent two devils to the inner cave to fetch Peleg, and when they opened the door they understood how it was with him and they turned grey and stood there abashed. Now Peleg had had plenty of time to collect himself and to consider what he would do and he was accustomed to the sight of fiends, however plain. He came at them briskly and struck their heads together for the glory of God so hard that they gave out a sound like a mallet on wood and no other but lay there like sacks. And he stepped over them and came to the outer cave where the captain of the devils was waiting and the Captain saw how it was with him and stood up, grey in his colour and shrinking. Peleg struck him down for the glory of the Trinity and bent him back so that his horns, which were his pride and joy, locked in the long curl of his hoofs, and Peleg bowled him in a hoop out of the cave and down the slope to a bottomless mere, where he lies still, mopping and mowing for ever in a powerful rage and heating the waters of the mere so that neither fish nor frog can live there, far less breed, whereas before it was the great place for the snigging of eels.

Then he took his cousin Kevin from the corner of the cave and asked had any of the other devils a word in their mouths, but they standing mumchance and looking meaner than any book can say he gave them all a great devastating curse and walked out into the light of the day.

He walked with his head in the air for seven miles, glorying in the verdant world and the blue of the sky and longing for some honest meat, and Kevin followed him with the meanness of hell showing in his face. Then Peleg remembered his humility and made Kevin go in front, and they came to the edge of a chasm. This chasm was a furlong across and far deeper and it barred their way, and as Peleg stood there on the edge considering it and marvelling at its black depth and the wafting fog in it Kevin thought of the thirty bags of gold and the life-long idleness and safety for ever that the oldest hob-devil had promised him by the holiest oath if he would do Peleg a mischief, and he considered too how that he was already damned for sure, and, trembling all over, he crept behind Peleg and with a desperate moan he hurled his weight on Peleg's back and Peleg fell with his two hands outstretched grasping the air.

Before Peleg had fallen a yard the fiends of hell were upon Kevin and they snatched him away to their own place, he screaming like a stuck pig about their oath and they laughing white-hot tongues of fire.

And the angel at the bottom of the chasm peered up through the shifting fog and altered his feet, and as he caught Peleg he said, 'There, easy now, Peleg.' And he put him down and looked kindly in his face and said, 'Sit down upon the flat rock, Peleg, for you are pale in the face, I find.' 'God put a flower on you, joy,' said Peleg, and thanked him with all the civility at his command and many elegant turns of speech.

The angel let him breathe awhile and said, 'Stand up now, Peleg, for I have a message for you. It is you must go down to the sea again, to the heathen of the pagan shore, and there are fourteen kings of the pagan shore to whom you must preach the faith, for now there is virtue in you. That is the message: and now we shall take a glass or two together, for I have a bottle conveniently near at hand, and it appears that I will not see you again until I stand with my trumpet to sound you in over the mossy walls of Paradise.'

A Passage of the Frontier

THE THREAT from the north grew stronger, and the stateless persons and undesirables began to move towards the Mediterranean and the southern frontiers. Then suddenly, overnight, the full danger was there, immediately at hand: blind tanks roared down the motorways, endless lines of trucks full of infantrymen, guns, the political police; and far ahead of them all parachutists were setting up road-blocks, directing the military traffic, requisitioning houses, carrying out the first arrests. All trains were stopped, all main roads, bridges, tunnels closed.

Now plans that needed more than a few hours for their execution were abandoned; now the nearest road was the only road; and before dawn on Friday a hired car put Martin down at the end of a charcoal-burner's track on the high slope of the Coma du Loup.

They would have preferred to get him out of the country by way of Switzerland, but that was impossible now: all frontiers were closed to those with no legal identity. Encantats was the only solution, a small Pyrenean smuggling centre inland from Andorra, even higher and more remote. It possessed no motor-road into France, but as even the mule-track was guarded they had him set down in the Coma du Loup with a drawing of the smugglers' path and a carrier-bag of food; and Jacob lent him a hard-weather coat. The driver also had an envelope of paper money, to be handed over at the last moment; but he did not see fit to hand it over – he turned his car, throwing up loose earth, bark and scraps of charcoal on the blackened ground. Martin made stiff, inadequate gestures to guide him – stiff because he was still cramped by the long night's headlong flight. The driver took no notice until the car was round; then he put his huge face out of the window, and through the smoke and steam he shouted, 'You follow the river. The ford is the boundary. Cross and follow the right-hand stream. You can't miss it.'

'Thank you very much,' said Martin. 'Good-bye.'

'The stream on the right,' said the driver, holding up his left hand. 'I've never been there myself, but you can't miss it.' He gave Martin a cold nod, crashed the gear home and jerked off down the track. The car was gone in a moment, but for some time it could still be heard, winding down through the trees in the darkness. Martin did not move until the sudden chatter of a jay startled him into motion, breaking a spell that might have lasted until the rising of the sun. He picked up his paper bag and began to climb through the trees.

This was near the top of the forest: he had passed up through the last half-mile of beeches, and now on the higher slope it was all pines, scaley pines standing steep from the mountainside. On his right hand the broad stream ran fast and deep, fall and pool, fall and pool all the way, and the brown water racing between high banks of rock.

At the beginning, under the beeches, there had been a clear path, indeed several paths; but up here the pine-needles did not hold the track. There were great heaps made by ants with wandering lines among them that might have been made by any number of beasts; but nothing like a distinct trail. The slope increased, and soon he was gasping; and as the day grew warmer, so green clouds of pollen began to drift through the forest, an enormous vegetable act of love. He came to a rocky shoulder where the trees grew sparse – no canopy to shut him in – and far over he saw the opposing mountain-flank, smoking green as though the whole forest were on fire.

In another hour he reached a level stretch of the river, a

place where he could reach the water and wash and drink at last. Drying, he sat on a grey boulder and picked raspberries. They grew all along among the rounded boulders, now that the trees were thinner, together with columbines and yellow lilies. Out there in the stream, where a fallen trunk had made an island, stood another lily, a tall purple spotted one whose petals curved back to touch its stem; and lying among the leaves at its foot, a blue crumpled packet that had held cigarettes. Nearer, in the gin-clear water, a rusting sardine-tin. 'Might this be the ford?' he said, and looked more attentively at the banks. Yes, certainly this was a place where one could cross, perhaps the first he had seen between the deep-cut banks; and certainly people had been crossing here for years and years, since the steep rock on the far bank was worn into steps. And farther up another stream joined this, as both the drawing and the driver had said.

So this was the frontier itself. He stepped into the water, unbelievably cold, and stood for a while with a foot on either side of the middle-line: then he waded over, to another country.

It feels much the same, however, he said, looking back to the bank he had left. The same trees over there, the same wild falls of rock, furred over with dry grey lichen; and a very small bird continually flitted to and fro across the water, busily from tree to tree, minding him no more than if he had been a cow.

Where it ran along the difficult course of the right-hand stream, the path was clear again; and often whole stretches of the bare mother-rock were trodden out into a smoothness that showed the grain and inner colour of the schist; but sometimes the steady upward sweep of the mountain was broken by broad level steps where the river soaked promiscuously among the bushes and the swampy earth, the coarse hummocks of grass and sour brown pools; here, and even more in the frequent steep gulleys, the path would divide, wander and dwindle into unmeaning ribbons. Yet time and again when he seemed to have lost it for ever his hand would reach out for a branch whose bark was already worn to the wood, or as he leapt a small ravine his foot would land in a place worn deep by other men. The path always reappeared, and it led him high, high towards the last thinning-out of the trees; now they stood wide apart, each one lower, with its underbranches touching the now frosty ground, and each looking older by far. The whole character of the forest had changed; the trees no longer hemmed him in, but stood casually, with junipers between them and even broad glades of low pink-flowering rhododendrons or open grass, studded with unopened gentians.

Then came one last belt of ancient twisted moss-clad pines, hardly more than bushes, and abruptly he was out of the trees altogether: they were ruled off as though by a line, and the sky, no longer patches of light above the branches, spread wide overhead. An enormous sky; vivid and brilliant beyond anything he had imagined: these hours of climbing had kept his head down, and now the immensity of this vast bowl overwhelmed him.

Another five hundred feet over the bare grass and he sat down to gaze round the world. His heart was pounding and his breath came short – visible breath that lingered in the unmoving, frigid air – and for some time his gasping body would scarcely let him comprehend what he saw: it was as though he were contemplating a brilliant but entirely foreign universe. Yet in time it resumed an intelligible form: there was his dark forest, sweeping down in wave after wave to the dim lower clouds; and beyond the great valley to the north rose answering mountains with rounded tops. Somewhere in the hidden land between them must be the last remote village and the road. It was an enormous landscape, on a scale that quite abolished hours or miles, but this was not the half of it – behind him the high mountain cut off the rest of the world. To his right as he turned there were two soaring peaks, joined by a ragged curtain-wall;

they were very dark on this northward side, and the snow that lay in their deep gulleys showed with a deathly light; they had screes and beds of shale hanging on their steep sides or running down to the chaotic rocks below, and the screes were cold and grey, severely inanimate. But on his left the solitary peak had caught the sun. Every detail of its warm brown and ochre cliffs was clear, and in this brilliant clarity it might have been no more than an hour away, but for the golden cloud that floated between him and the nearest spur. Between these mountains, and due south of him, there appeared the upward edge of a wilderness of rock that threw up uncounted peaks; their grey northern sides were powdered with snow, and deep snow lay here and there in streaks. These raised, distant peaks were all he could see of the waste beyond. 'The necessary pass will be clear, no doubt,' he said, 'once I can survey the whole.'

The cold seeped into him from below; the air bit his ears and nose; and when at last he felt for the map his hands were numb. The single mountain was certainly Malamort, and it was beyond it, on the sunward side, that he must go, through a gap between the mountain and the chaos to the south: he could see no gap, but his drawing showed the path, a line winding up to the shoulder of Malamort. The gap must be there, and it must be exactly to the south-east, hidden by some nearer crest. With a sudden eager desire to know what was on the other side of the limiting ridge, to find the pass, to be moving in this silent enormous world, he started up the slope, a smooth alp dotted with pale boulders like gigantic sheep.

It was a rounded slope whose skyline mounted pace by pace with him, false crests in an interminable series, and it was steep; yet he hurried up it, sometimes chuckling, sometimes singing loud; and where the slope was less he ran in bounds, waving his arms and singing louder still. The grass thinned and the bare earth showed more as he gained height, gritty earth among pale grass, dirty and crushed

from the snow that had left it a few days ago. Now and
then he slipped and fell; but he fell easy on the wet sloping
ground; it did not affect his elation nor his speed and in
time he gained the true ridge at last, with its long wave of
standing snow. Here he fell silent: now he was standing in the
sun, astride of a vaster world by far, because the last two
thousand feet had brought up mountains on every hand,
and he was above them all, above everything except
Malamort; and clean round the horizon these mountains
rose and fell, a brown infinity. The great valley on the north
was gone, obliterated by the miracle of breeding cloud,
rounded white masses rising below him into the middle air,
forming slow whirlpools and momentary towers. Once the
whole gleaming ocean parted from top to bottom, and
he saw a heightened fragment of the common world –
thread-like roads, the railway-line, a winding river, the
huddle of a town with smoke, the minute patchwork of
fields. But with the closing of the clouds and their continual
mounting there was nothing on that side but the great
ranges as they stretched away, illimitable against the lower
sky, rising from the rising sea of white: but on this side, the
new, southern, sunlit side, no clouds; nothing but a desert
of broken rock, brilliantly lit yet dark and even black in
places, with sheets of snow and many lakes, black-rimmed,
shining water in the hollows; screes everywhere, and rarely
a touch of green. The wilderness filled all the middle
distance, and beyond it the saw-edged ranges ran on and
on: the mountains of Aragon, no doubt, and perhaps those
of Navarre.

The snow under his feet was crusted, granular and hard;
it was pocked with old rain and powdered with a dust of
earth, but beneath the crust it was the purest white. Its
taste was thin – insubstantial – yet it left a burning in his
mouth.

Virgin snow: there seemed a want of piety in walking
upon its unbroken smoothness; and never was there such a

world for piety – it might have been created yesterday. Others had not felt the same, however. Twenty yards away to the left footmarks crossed it at its lowest point. What is more, they continued beyond the present limit of the snow; and these compressed footprints were still unmelted; they ran on, a series of white dots pointing straight to a cleft under the sheer rock-face of Malamort, a slit perhaps an hour away, hardly to be seen at all in the blaze of the sun without their help. For this necessary pass, this Portal Nera, lay in the deep shadow among black, impassable rocks.

Once he was across and fairly on the southern slope, the sun warmed him through and through, comforting him to the bone. The gentians were open here, stars and trumpets, fields of them, and the air was like good news: he said, I could go on for ever.

He walked with long, reaching strides, on and on: yet the sun climbed and the pass barely moved. The air was stirring now, and a black vulture rose in spirals on a thermal current until it was no bigger than a lark: the bowl of the sky turned an even intenser blue. This was perfect walking, these miles of level or slightly downward path, almost like a slow gentle flight or even levitation after the grind of the ascent: slowly the pass changed shape, and to his left the peak soared higher still, growing until it filled the eastern quarter of the sky.

For long stretches he watched the alternate reappearance of his feet and the even flow of the ground beneath. Once he looked up at the clatter of a band of chamois crossing a scree a mile away to the west, and once he followed the flight of a large white butterfly with red eye-spots on its wings; but upon the whole he kept his head down, in a floating dream.

The third time he looked up he was in the very entrance of the pass, and he saw a man in a grey cloth cap, a surly red-eyed man with his legs wrapped in coarse brown paper from knee to ankle: he was sitting on a dark boulder in the shadow of the cliff, beside a shapeless load, or burden. He asked Martin had he the right time?

'I am afraid I have not,' said Martin, 'but it is early yet, I am sure.' He sat down and watched the man as he knotted two broken ends in the sacking of his load.

'Whore of Babylon,' said the man, forcing the knots tight; and he muttered continually as he turned the bundle over and over to verify the fastenings. 'What is your name?' he asked.

'Martin Kaftan.'

'Where do you come from?'

'France.'

'Where are you going? Are you alone? Do you know anyone in Encantats?'

Martin answered these questions, and after a pause the man, pretending to inspect his burden still, drew out a knife. He feigned to cut the loose end of a string and said, 'You know nothing about the mountain. Look at your shoes. I dare say you have a good many pairs of leather shoes in your house,' he added, with a cunning leer. Martin looked at his shoes: their soles were shining from the grass; they were indeed quite unsuitable. 'Come,' said the man, 'let me scratch them with my knife.'

With the shoes in front of him he did not scratch them yet, but pushed up his sleeve and began to shave the hair on his forearm. The hairs skipped under the edge, leaving a bare, mown tract of skin. 'Sharp,' he said. 'That's what I call sharp.' He was looking uglier now, with white spittle between his lips, his eyes were squinting with excitement, and the defect in his speech grew more pronounced. He said, 'You are afraid to be on the mountain alone with all that money and your fine coat. Let me feel your coat. What have you got to eat?'

Martin laughed, leaning back against the rock. He said, 'How would I be afraid on the mountain, my dear? And no one can rob me on this journey, because I was robbed before

I began. The coat is not mine, and I left all my food at the top of the forest, by mistake: a chicken, bread, and a bottle of wine. What is your name, pray?'

'Joan,' said the man, vaguely. He seemed to be coming out of his fit, and although he said 'No,' when Martin asked him whether he had anything to eat either, after a little while he brought out a flat black loaf and two onions and unslung the greasy leather bottle he wore on his shoulder. He scratched a cross on the loaf, cut off a piece and gave it to Martin with one of the onions; and when Martin held out his hand for the knife to slice the onion he passed it without reflection. He also passed the wine.

Munching fast he told Martin how good he was: uniquely good: took no advantage of the situation as any other man might, nay *would,* for the laws of God were not observed and God Himself had never reached these parts. 'There was the izard-hunter from Politg – they cut his throat in this very pass before he could say hail Mary and Espollabalitris ate his balls.'

'What are izards?'

'Izards are what you make chamois-skin out of: where were you brought up, God forbid? But I should never have eaten any Christian's balls. I am too good,' he said with his eyes closed tight, and he pressed Martin to eat more, to drink as much as he could. 'Drink, man, drink. I do not reckon the cost,' he said, squirting the jet into Martin's mouth.

'You are very kind,' said Martin, when the skin was empty. 'I hope you will find my chicken, in time, and the bottle. They are in a paper carrier-bag, on a rock where the trees begin.'

'Never mind, never mind if the bears have had them. I can go on all day and night without refreshment, to help a poor man. I do good, but I never mention it. There are hundreds and thousands down there' – jerking his head backwards – 'who owe everything to me: but I say nothing.'

93

Shading his mouth he whispered, 'There are evil tongues down there,' and nodding vehemently he set to scratching the shoes, raising diagonal weals on their soles with the point of his knife.

'Thank you very much,' said Martin, making to put them on.

'No, no. Let me,' cried Joan, cramming them on to Martin's feet and lacing them with terrible force. He grew excited again when he described the course of the path as it led on to the Cami Real, the great mule-track, confused in his description, obscurely angry and contentious; his ugliness was increasing fast, but when Martin said he supposed the burden must weigh a great deal Joan turned off directly to tell what he could carry, compared with common men. And indeed when Martin lifted it, meaning to help it on, the weight was staggering. Joan thrust him aside, swung it up with one hand, looped it on with a sordid web and stood displaying himself with angry satisfaction. 'Watch me,' he cried, setting off at a furious pace up the hill. His voice came fainter: 'You have never seen anything like it. But this is nothing to what I can do, Mother of God.'

'Thank you for telling me the way,' Martin called after him; but Joan ran on and on, without another word.

For two hours more the path ran sweetly round the shoulder of Malamort, dipping to a lake: other paths had joined it, coming from valleys to the east, but they were obviously less important; and in any event this lake was marked upon his drawing: it had been named by Joan. All that he had to do now was to walk left-handed round its shore, climb by the stream the other side, reach the high snowy ridge beyond, find the westward pass above two small lakes, and so drop to the road.

The great hollow, a ring two miles across, was surrounded by cliffs on three sides; they had beds of shale at their feet, and in three places they were broken by streams coming from the higher ridge. Three streams, and one of them a waterfall; yet clearly the first was his. It was much larger; it was directly on the other side of the lake; and there had been no mention of his crossing water.

The fourth side was filled by a marsh, covered with cotton-grass, and among the boulders on its edge grew a low, fern-like plant in great profusion; the last year's growth, brown, dry in the sun, and fragrant, made the softest resting-place. He sat down and gazed at the water, his whole body relaxing at once, limp, boneless and pliable: the lake had no banks, in the ordinary sense – there were just these falls of rock, and then, without transition, water. It had no vegetation in it or round it: no clouds passed overhead, no birds. No breeze touched its surface. It seemed that there was no life here, only sky, rock and silence; but presently he saw rings spreading, and later he heard the splash of a rising trout. There were other sounds too: stone avalanches rumbling in the distance; the thunder of rock falling from the cliffs, several times repeated, and startling at first. He watched the rings form, spread and intersect; he dozed, awoke, dozed again, and fell fast asleep in his bed of fern.

It was a nearer rock-fall and the cold that roused him. The sun had left the water, the whole bottom of the ring, and now it lit only the upper half of the eastern cliff: already the air down here was sharp. There was no time to be lost, and quickly putting on his shoes he hurried round the lake. He climbed fast up along the bed of the first stream, but the shadow climbed faster still: before he had reached the ridge the lower sky was violet, and the arch of the day was closing towards the west. He had seen nothing like a path for the last hour, but now the snow was coming closer, and surely he would find it there.

Indeed, there it was, a track slanting westwards across the snow, almost exactly where his anxious theory had placed it. But alas, when he came to it there was clearly something wrong – too slender, far too neat – and when he bent in the fading light he saw the mark of cloven hoofs. This was the path, and no doubt the habitual path, of a numerous band of chamois. Certainly it was: ten minutes later he rounded a bluff with the breeze in his face and came full upon them. The group exploded, racing away, leaping skip-skip-skip down and across an impossible rock-face, so that he was in dread for their legs and necks.

However, they were gone, safely gone, before he could even count them, and his anxiety returned to himself; the twilight was mounting fast to these regions, and the only hint of real path that he could see led upwards, still higher, to no pass that he could discern among the massive peaks ahead.

'Yet it may very well drop again suddenly,' he said. 'It may very well show me the pass in half an hour; and as soon as I am on the road I shall find a shepherd's hut. Joan spoke of one where the road leaves the forest, and two not far from the chapel.'

On. Higher and higher, winding where the rocks would let him rather than where a fading sense of direction urged him to go. He often fell now, once losing his hold on a scree and sliding down a hundred feet with stones falling all around and beyond him. Eventually, with his breath gone, his strength going, and a deep cut in his side, he found himself creeping in the near darkness along a snowy ledge with a sheer face on his right hand and a precipice on his left.

The snow had melted away from the rock-face, where the sun had warmed it, leaving a passage wide enough to stand in – wider in places – and then, on the outward side of the ledge, a firm white mass as high as a counter. He leant on this counter, surveying the night as it rose from the east – Mars blazing already, even the small stars pricking out, but never a hint of the moon – and the dark shapes of the mountains looming against the sky. 'I am far, far too high,' he said. 'But I cannot go any farther. Snow is said to conserve the warmth: I shall try to find a wider place, and there I shall lie.'

Fifty yards along the ledge turned sharply: he was observing, 'And if it does not, then I shall run up and down until the day,' when he heard a snort, a muffled, hurrying sound ahead. At the same moment he caught a goatish smell, and his feet were treading in dung. 'So this is where the chamois sleep,' he said. 'How wise.'

It was the most sheltered place that could be wished at this great height: beneath the counter there was no wind at all; some warmth still emanated from the cliff, and the smell soon passed unnoticed. His body was so tired that the rock seemed soft at first, and he lay there in a half-doze, watching the stars as they swept over the narrow trench above.

A long, long night, however, with an increasing cold that reached to his heart at last. By two o'clock it seemed to have been going on for ever. But at least he was beyond hunger, and his thirst he could satisfy from the snow. When the stars were paling he fell into a tormented sleep, cramped and uneasy, but so deep that the sun was as high as the Malamort before it woke him.

'It is over,' he said, shading his eyes from the glare and unscrewing himself from the tight ball in which he had lain. 'It is over at last.' He got on to his knees, then to his feet, and as he slowly straightened so the pure revivifying sunlight darted straight into his upper half: his blood began to flow, the tension and shivering died away as the heat pierced deeper and deeper; his teeth no longer chattered. He took off his soaking bloodstained filthy coat and stood back against the warm rock with his arms spread wide and his eyes closed. All around him there was the drip of melting snow.

Now his shirt was dry and even his frozen spine was supple; he leant his elbows on the counter and looked out. Below him, cloud. Nothing but that white sea of impenetrable cloud, rising to within five hundred feet of his ledge.

Mountains thrusting through it – to his left the familiar praying hands of Malamort – and a perfect sky above. He said, 'They will lift in time,' and his eye caught a white-splashed shelf of rock below, within spitting distance below. Three bearded vultures stood upon it, the parents and their huge blowzy child, sluggishly preening themselves and waiting for the day to warm. His gaze made them uneasy, and presently one cocked its head upwards, shuffled to the edge and launched itself silently into the void. The others followed, and for a moment he saw six great sharp-winged forms gliding over the clouds, the birds and their close-following shadows.

'I have slept with vultures too, I find,' he observed; and wedging its sleeves into a horizontal crack he spread his coat to dry.

There was no attempting to move except upwards, which was absurd; so during the hours in which the cloud slowly boiled and rolled in upon itself below, sometimes sending off long streamers but never breaking, he also dried his trousers and his handkerchief, luxuriating in the heat as they hung.

Gradually the unseen waterfall to his right increased in sound and volume as the sun unlocked the higher snow and ice; and when at last the cloud began its definitive rise, the jet came into sight, a single arch of water shooting out from a broken cliff and plunging into the whiteness, now only a hundred feet below.

Tenuous vapours were drifting overhead: all the sharp definition of the cloud was gone. The sun dimmed, and a moment later it was no more than a white ball in the enveloping fog. He put on his good dry clothes, grateful for their warmth, and relapsed into timeless waiting.

Would the cloud continue to rise? Or would it hang about the mountain-tops all day, all night, perhaps for weeks on end? A small shining beetle climbed laboriously about the pellet-shaped droppings and the compacted masses of izards' dung. Several times it fell on its back, waving its legs, and each time he set it on its feet; but it seemed to possess no sense of purpose or direction.

The cloud lifted. It took a great while to do so, but it lifted, and the last stage was as dramatic as the raising of a curtain. A hint of thinning, and then suddenly it was overhead, completely overhead, revealing the lower world, whole, clear and plain.

There, immediately below him, was the forest. There, on the flank of a valley, was the road, rising to a saddle to the west. There was the river. And there, on the grassy slopes above the forest, he could see minute shapes that must be grazing cattle. Poring over this landscape spread below him he made out three shepherd's huts, all far away, the nearest being close to the upper limit of the trees, between the forest and the road, on the far side of the river. From one blue smoke was rising; and each had a strange brown square in front of it, like a field.

There too were the small lakes, far away to the east; and there to be sure he saw the path, so well trodden by the herds down there that it might have been a road. He had not gone so far wrong: the general direction had been right. Only he was three thousand feet too high. And his precipice fell half that distance without a break. How to get down it? Along the ledge in the hope of its joining that far shoulder? Back the way he had come, trusting to find a way along its foot? There were not so many hours of daylight left, with the tall mountains cutting off the sun so soon, and the best way he must find, or he was lost in sight of home.

Backwards, forwards, sideways, up and down, climbing, sliding, sometimes falling, it was not until the evening sky flushed red that he was down to the two small lakes, fetching them at last by a long tack that lost him an hour and more. 'But once I am round this pool,' he said, forcing his exhausted body through a bog, 'I am certainly on the one true path: then if I do not fall again I may very well get there by night. And surely I shall not fall upon the road itself?'

Five minutes later he missed his leap on a shifting rock; but the fall sent him sprawling on to the undoubted path, and now it was only a question of clearing his head, gathering himself together, choosing the right direction, and going on and on for some hours. 'Providing the shepherd is at home,' he said.

Past the lakes, on, and a long haul, to the first of the trees, strangely familiar with their hanging moss in the deepening twilight; down through the trees to the river and the ford. The swift icy current, knee-deep and more; the slippery stones in the darkness. He said, 'Shall I ever make this last half-mile?' as he paused long on the farther bank, searching for strength to stand up again. There was only a plain meadow between him and the light of the open door, but now the cruel frost came dropping from the sky and he was as weary as a dying man.

Ahead of him stood the herd, packed into the trampled square in front of the hut – mares with their mule foals, cows, heifers, beasts, some sheep, two goats, two pigs, with a mist of soft breath rising from them all – a guardian dog at each corner, huge woolly dogs with steel-spiked brass collars. They had heard and smelt him coming since before he crossed the river, but they said nothing: only one young subsidiary dog slunk close behind his legs and gibbered its teeth uneasily; and he walked very slowly past them towards the door.

It was open to let out some of the smoke, and it showed a glowing stone-built room. There were two fires blazing inside, one on the hearth, another, a small and clear fire of juniper, burning on a stone shelf beside the bench; and this bench, this broad wooden platform against the back wall, filled the entire width of the hut. The shepherd lay there on a deep pile of sheepskins, and he was reading in a book. One arm held it to the light, and the other lay round the lamb that slept against his side. A very old bitch and some cats filled the rest of the bed.

The very old bitch grunted as Martin appeared in the door, and the shepherd turned his eager smiling face towards him. 'Have you come?' he said, closing the book, disengaging the lamb, and beginning to rise. 'And have you come at last? You are the Christ? I have been waiting and waiting for you.'

'No, my dear,' said Martin, leaning against the jamb. 'I am not the Christ.'

'Are you not?' said the shepherd, touching his arm. His face clouded painfully; but he said, 'Lie down on the warm bed, while I milk a cow.' He looked searchingly into Martin's face again and said, 'And are you indeed not the Christ? Yet the dogs never spoke; and this is the time. No? Well,' – smiling once more – 'then I shall not have to kill the lamb.'

The Voluntary Patient

'WHAT is that noise?'

'Which noise?'

'Like a dog howling. There it is again.'

'Oh, that. It is only Mr Philips. He is upstairs this afternoon,' she said with a satisfied smile. 'We have been a little
troublesome, and we shan't come down until we are in a
better mood. "You can't do this to me," he says, "I am here
on a voluntary basis, you understand, and can leave whenever I choose, upon giving proper notice." '

They both laughed, and the second woman, still tittering,
said, 'Always the same old tale. But which is Mr Philips?
The one who looks out of the window?'

'No. Isn't he a scream? No, this is the one with the fiddle
I told you about. You haven't seen him yet – he is at the
back.'

'Well, why doesn't he play his fiddle?'

'He has quite given it over, and spends all his time
writing. I said to him the other day, "Mr Philips," I said,
"why don't you give us a tune?" No answer. Just scribble
scribble scribble, as if his life depended on it.'

They both laughed again, and the second woman said,
'You get all the funny ones.'

'Not that he's as funny as some, but he does get some
funny ideas. "Make the punishment fit the crime" is his
latest.' She hummed a bar and they both sang.

> 'La di da di da di da
> Make the punishment fit the crime.'

'How do you mean, though?' asked the visitor.

103

'Well, he says all this psychosomatic stuff – you know what I mean?'

'Of course I do.'

'Don't be offended, love. He says it is all part of the same thing, and you bring it on yourself.' The visitor grinned and nodded, and the tall, black-haired woman went on, 'It's all part of the same thing, he says. Oh, we get it by the hour sometimes, and then he writes it all down.'

'You do have more fun than we do,' said the visitor crossly. 'On the accidie side they are a dull, mumchance, pompous lot, all puffed up with their own importance.'

'Oh, I don't know,' said the other in a modest tone. 'Here,' she added, leaning sideways and picking up a closely written sheet, 'this will tell you all about it. It will make you howl.'

The visitor, a woman with sparse sandy hair and a dead-white transparent skin, flushed so that the redness could be seen mounting above the rounded protuberance of her forehead and far into her scalp. She took it greedily, but she said at once, 'This is not the beginning.'

'It doesn't matter: it's all the same.'

' "... and as no two crimes are exactly the same," ' she read aloud, ' "so every punishment is unlike every other punishment. When a man wakes in the night and finds his head filled with remorse and bitter, old regret, if he chose he could reflect that no other man in the world would be suffering precisely that remorse nor exactly that regret: it might be quite as vain and sterile and long-lived, but it would not be wounding him with the same sharp terms. Of course, he would not choose to do so, for he would be too busy dodging about inside his mind, trying to escape – unless, that is, he were occupied with feeling the wound to see how much it still hurt and trying to persuade himself that there was virtue in mere remorse." He, he, he,' went the sandy woman; but putting her glass on the paper she said with an affected prim indifference, 'He writes very neat.'

'I don't know that that's the best piece,' said the other, peering at the writing upside down. 'There was a good one I meant to show you the day before yesterday.'

'From Mr Philips?'

'No, the pale fellow.'

'He's another funny one, isn't he?' she said abstractedly, as her eyes ran down the paragraph below the round of the glass's foot.

' "So in sinning you create your own punishment," ' she read. ' "In the act of the particular and unique sin the compensating punishment is born: it is inevitably born, and it always exactly counterbalances its cause." '

'Does he ever put any address?' she asked, breaking off.

'No: he's one of our new boys. They haven't let on yet.'

'Has he told you what his trouble is?'

'No. But you would have screamed the other day: they were asking him about his eyes and I couldn't help hearing. Osborne says, "And what about this shadow in the left-hand field of vision, Mr Philips?" And he says, "Oh, it's nothing much." So Osborne says, "But it is still there, I collect?" And he says, "I'm afraid so. Do you attach any importance to it?" – trying to put him off, you know. Then Osborne hums and haws about sciasis for a bit, tips old Prince the wink, and leaves them together. Old Prince, of course, begins to lay on the soothing syrup right away – dear, kind old man, butter wouldn't melt in his mouth.'

Both the women laughed, slapping their thighs and rocking to and fro. The dark one controlled herself first and said, 'A drop more, love?'

'I don't mind if I do,' she said, holding her fingers to the glass. 'Ta.'

At this moment the black-haired woman was called out of the room and the visitor, dangling her tongue into her gin, but not sipping it, read on over the rim of her glass.

"It is not the observer who must be asked, but the sufferer. To the observer it must appear that there are many identical crimes, which may or may not have identical punishments. If we take the ordinary crimes, lying and theft, it can be said that in every case the criminal is punished by being a liar (for obviously it is not the punishment of being dis-believed that counts – that is no more than a haphazard retribution for lack of skill) or by being a thief, by inhabiting the mind and body of a thief: but that is a merely superficial view. Take as an example the commonest criminal of them all, the selfish, disagreeable man: this sufferer, heavy under the self-inflicted punishment of an everlasting evil temper fixed into his body by his indulgence in unpleasantness, can point out a thousand significant differences in his punishment as compared with the next man's; the weight of his sour life presses on innumerable points of sensitivity that no other man can have. It is the same with the ordinary hysterias, neuroses, and psychosomatic diseases. Yet it is true that in this range we do have an apparent similarity: the enormous differences, the differences that instantly convince the most casual observer, come from huge and monstrous crimes. It is these that cause the monstrous births upon the other side. I think of the horrible thing at the bottom of the Last Judgment at Albi: that must have been created, automatic-ally created, by one appalling crime alone. That crime may have been called by the same name as other crimes (Judas' sin is nominally shared by the latest petty traitor) but obviously it was as unique as its result. This thing at Albi could never possibly have served to counterweigh two crimes: it was made by one alone. Bosch and Breughel, too; they show the harmony and equipoise . . ."

Her eyes skipped down the lines until a capital began again. "It comes to this: each of these acts adds another to those things that live in Hell – *creates* it. It creates a new fiend." A pleased smile spread slowly across her face: she nodded her head, staring intently at the blank wall in front of her.

'What was it?' she asked, as the door opened again.

'Oh, nothing. Only the brimstone going out. But as I was saying, old Prince sits himself down and goes on and on in his quiet, soapy voice – gets very confidential and friendly.'

'He is a proper card, old Prince.'

'Yes. He likes to see how far he can make them go. If only he can get them to go down on their knees and blubber the whole thing out while he does you know what behind them, it sets him up for a fortnight. Sometimes he borrows Ambrose's outfit, but the pure jam is when he can firk it out of them voluntary, sobbing in mother-bull's bosom. Anyhow, this time he gets our gentleman on to his hobby-horse about this psychosomatic business and rewards and punishments and so on; then after a bit he breaks off and says, "But this figure that you think you see, Mr Philips, it has no certain form?"

' "No!" he says, as quick as that. Then he hesitates and says, "No. No. It is only dark. Always behind me, as I told you; and when I turn it goes."

' "It always goes? Vanishes?"

' "Yes."

' "Always?"

' "Yes. Well, that is to say . . ." He hesitates, and old Prince looks grave and sympathetic, very interested and kind. ". . . that is to say, almost always. But once I turned too quick and I thought I saw it then."

' "Was it – forgive me if I seem indelicate – was it a dreadful thing?"

' "I hardly know what to say," says Mr Philips, pretending to blow his nose and dropping his handkerchief. "Not really, perhaps. Not in itself. I thought it was the shadow of a barn – the sharp line and the corner."

' "Just that? No more than that?"

' "The shadow of a barn. The side going up so sheer and the angle of the roof."

'Old Prince leans back in his chair, looks at his watch, and coughs. "Shadows, my dear sir," he says, rather impatient but covering it up, you see . . .'

'He's a cunning one, old Prince.'

' ". . . shadows," he says. "We all know how a horse will shy. We all know, too, how our bodies can deceive us, and especially our eyes. An unwise indulgence, a late supper, and we are apt to dream at night and to have our faculties disturbed the next day. Singing in the ears, spots floating in the air. They tell me it is the liver." And he looks at his watch again. But our Mr P. is getting very agitated, gripping the arms of his chair so that the whole floor trembles.

' "Don't go," he cries – as if old Prince had any intention of going – "I should like to . . ." He bogs down there; but after a minute he says, "I had an interesting talk with Father Ambrose the other day."

' "Oh indeed?" says Prince, very solemn. "Well, I am sure it must have done you good. My dear colleague has a brilliant understanding: I only wish he could be here more often. But they keep him so very busy, you know."

' "Your colleague? But I thought you were . . ."

' "Why, yes. Father Ambrose is my colleague. In my humble way I fulfil a dual function here. I am very proud of my connection with him: he is a wonderful person, and I have learned a great deal from him. I am sure he must have done you good?"

' "Yes, yes," he says, "Father Ambrose was very kind – wonderfully patient – most considerate."

' "May I ask what you talked about?"

' "It was mostly the same subject that we have just been discussing. But he is so sympathetic that I ventured to put it on a personal plane."

' "I see. I see. You told him everything?"

' "Yes."

' "Everything?"

' "Yes."

' "So of course he was able to reassure you completely?"

' "It was not a regular confession, you understand," says Mr P., still holding off.

' "No. I quite understand. But, however, he was able to reassure you."

' "Yes."

'I thought that was the end, but after a while old Prince leans forward and says, "My dear Philips – I hope you do not mind me calling you that – my dear Philips, I am afraid that you may have some unexpressed reserve. Unfortunately Father Ambrose will not be back for some considerable time, but if I can be of any service to you, I am entirely at your disposition."

' "It was *after* my talk with him that I turned and saw it clearly," blurts out Mr Philips.

' "Dear me," cries Prince, and I knew he was so near a fit of the giggles that I nearly went off myself, although I was alone in the corridor. But he goes on very grave and earnest. "Dear me, you must have found that very disturbing."

' "I can't bear it. I can't bear it," he says.

' "Now, now, my dear Philips; let us be calm. Calm. I am here to help you: you know that, don't you? Let us look at it this way: as it happened after you had had your, your 'talk' shall we say, with Father Ambrose, there cannot possibly be any connection between this and your former – what term shall we employ? – your former visions. For as I understand it you told Father Ambrose *everything*? The account was quite complete?"

' "Yes. But perhaps it was not valid."

' "If it was complete it was certainly valid. There were no omissions?"

' "Oh no. Certainly not – no voluntary omission at all."

' "Perhaps some little suppression almost unnoticed at the time, which has occurred to you since?"

' "I don't think so. No. But I can't bear it – I can't. It is getting so much worse."

'Prince calms him down a little and then says, "Perhaps if we were to run over the main points of your conversation with Father Ambrose you might find it helpful, and it is possible that you might bring something fresh into your memory, something that you unconsciously kept in the background before. As I am sure you have noticed, our memories are extraordinarily unreliable, and they have a strange capacity for hiding things that we do not wish to remember. Yes, I am sure that that would be our best course: but may I beg you to be frank? I am sure that you will realize that complete frankness is of the first importance."

' "You are very kind. But I am afraid of trespassing on your good nature. I kept Father Ambrose here for hours."

' "Not at all, not at all. Now I think – yes, I am sure of it. I think you would be more at your ease if you were to kneel here, facing the window. I shall be able to hear you perfectly well. Remember, you cannot be too minutely detailed."

'So Philips gets down on the floor and puts his face against the cushion of the chair old Prince has been sitting in and old Prince stands behind him in the middle of the room, bending up and down on his knees and going like *that* with his hands.'

'He, he, he.'

'But instead of beginning, he jumps up again and says, "Do you feel that my theory of punishment is sound, Mr Prince?"

' "Eh?" says old Prince, rather put out and giving him a dirty look under his eyebrows. He hadn't expected that, and nor had I; but he recovers himself and says, "A very interesting theory, Mr Philips, very interesting indeed. But these are terribly difficult questions and I am sure that our best course is to do as I suggested. Shall we begin at the beginning?"

'Of course, he wants to get him down on his knees again, and for a moment he does go down. But then he bobs up again and stands there wringing his hands as good as a play. "I can't bear it," he keeps saying, "I can't bear it."

' "There now, my dear Philips, let us collect ourselves. Let us be calm. I will be just here behind you, and I will listen without interruption, I assure you. And we must bear in mind the absolute necessity for complete frankness, must we not?"

'Old Prince is looking very ugly, but Philips is half turned to the window and doesn't see a thing: he keeps moaning "I can't bear it. I can't. I can't."

'Prince sees that it is no good going on with that line, so he hands him back into his chair, waits until he has come off the boil, and then, after a little while, he says in a thoughtful voice, "The shadow of an upright wall, and the angle of the roof. Now let us reflect. What, by your theory, could have called that into being?"

' "It is not only the line and corner now. I didn't tell you. I didn't like to say," he gasps.

' "There is something else?" murmurs old Prince, to help him on.

'Philips whispers something, but what it was I could not catch: the next thing is old Prince saying, "Perhaps you could give me a general idea, eh?"

'But "I can't name it," he says, jerking his head over his shoulder.

' "Just some hint – ?" says old Prince, for our man is very near the point now, and old Prince is all hot and excited. But it won't do: he has pressed him just an inch too far and at that point our man sticks. He can't bring it out, and it's no use, although Prince soothes him and soft-soaps him for half an hour and more. You would have screamed. If you had been there I would never have been able to hold out.'

'Was he cross?'

'He was livid, my dear. He got out of the room all right

in the end, still the dear old gentleman; but he gave me such a look as he shoved by.'

'He doesn't like to fail. But he'll have him next time.'

'Oh yes, he'll have him next time. But he likes it first go off, and this was rather a special one.'

'I wish I had seen it.' She paused for a while before adding, 'You have all the funny ones.'

'We've been lucky recently. There's another comic in the upper wing who – '

'What was that noise?'

'Which noise?'

'Like a dog howling.'

They both listened. The inhuman cry swelled to an enormous volume and after an instant's silence a furious trampling shook the ceiling of the room.

A slight frown creased the forehead of the black-haired woman, and she stood up, very tall and solid over the rickety table. 'The students?' she said. She stood considering for a moment with her lips pursed, while the hellish din continued overhead. 'Yes, the young devils must be teasing him. Old Prince said he might give them leave.'

A moment later she said, 'They've left him now.' She turned to a cupboard, took an instrument out for herself and handed another to the visitor.

'We'll go up too, shall we?' she said.

'Oh *yes*,' cried the other, jumping full of glee, 'and we'll make him say who created *us*.'

And laughing they hurled themselves out of the room and raced up the stairs, screaming with laughter that flew before them to the door of Mr Philips' private room.

The Long Day Running

————◆◆◆————

THE FIRST SONG Lemuel Kirk ever learnt was John Peel;
he loved everything about it; he knew all the words, and
he often made the palm-trees tremble with his view halloo.
He had longed to go out with a fell-pack from his earliest
days; and now that he was settled in Wales he had the
opportunity of fulfilling this ambition – indeed, of surpassing
it, for the country inland was made up not of fells but of
mountains.

His predecessor at the hospital, a Welshman with a wide
acquaintance in the surrounding counties, gave him an
introduction to the master of a famous old pack that hunted
them, and in the autumn a postcard came to tell Dr Kirk
that hounds would meet at Hafod Uchaf on Thursday, at
half past nine.

The dogs were a mixed body – fell-hounds, Welsh hounds,
a beautiful English bitch from the Pytchley, and almost as
many terriers as foxhounds: small terriers of different
colours, most of them whiskered and hairy, all coupled with
heavy chains. The Master was followed by a personal dog,
an old cross-bred black retriever that farted every few
minutes and that took no notice of anyone. The Master
himself was a spare, remote man with a hawk nose, a
curling moustache and a piercing blue eye: his horn could
be seen under his Burberry and he carried a long-lashed
crop slung over his shoulder. Something had occurred to
vex him, which disturbed the rest of the field; but he greeted
Kirk kindly, and hoped that they would be able to show

him some sport. Gerallt Williams, the huntsman, had brought his son to the hospital for a course of treatment, and Kirk already knew him. And there was a weather-beaten woman whom he recognized as one of the magistrates who had fined him for a motoring offence in the summer. The rest of the field he had never seen, to his knowledge: some local farmers and artisans; a tall soldier called Major Boyd, some other 'educated' men; a schoolmaster with a hard-faced virgin at his side. They were all dressed in strong, shabby clothes; they all wore boots; they all carried sticks. Kirk felt too new altogether, except for his boots – they at least had seen service during his long walks in August and September.

Little did Kirk know about hunting, and the apparent competence of the others disturbed him. Following at all seemed to him to imply a moral duty to keep up, to go through thick and thin, and to be in at the kill. He could not possibly expect to distinguish himself in any way, still less to be given a brush; but he did hope to avoid disgrace. He was the only black man in those parts; and apart from that these people seemed to him stand-offish – it would be painful to expose himself in front of them. Yet perhaps this was no more than a question of language: many of the patients from the hill farms and villages needed a Welsh-speaking nurse to interpret for them when it came to the finer points; and in his farther walks he had noticed how people avoided conversation, not to display their imperfect English.

At this point the farmers were all speaking Welsh – the word *llwynog* kept recurring; the Master spoke Welsh or English indifferently when he spoke at all. 'For Christ's sake let's cut the cackle, Dwch anwyl,' he said, pulling a watch from his waistcoat. 'If he don't choose to meet my bloody hounds prompt, let him go and – himself.'

They moved off, the huntsman; the lean pale pack,

smelling strong of hound; the Master and his familiar spirit, farting as it went; the shabby field.

As they came into the high valley, the fox slipped up over the edge of it and away. He went with no hurry, picking the easy path through rocks and shadows, and if it had not been for two sheep that started violently, making the shale rattle on the mountainside, he would never have been seen. A big dog-fox, long-legged and uncommonly dark: he paused on the skyline, on the edge of the steep slope, and looked down before he vanished.

There were half a dozen of them there at the far end of the lake and more strung out along its barren shore, all staring up at him: the hounds were farther on, where a fall came down to the water at the head of the valley. It made no difference to the fox that he had been seen, because the dogs were already working along his drag among the black rocks; but it pleased the followers – Kirk's heart leapt with delight.

This was Cwm Llyn Du, a great bowl of a valley like a crater with a quarter of its wall broken away at the lower end; it had high steep sides, so sheer that on the two arms before the break the grass could only just get a footing, while the top end was savage, bare and sterile.

The pack was on the true line, with Bashful and Melody out in front; and its meandering path showed exactly the way the fox had gone up some hours before. This was a fair scenting day up here, and suddenly as they came to the place where he had been lying, Melody bawled out with passionate conviction, then four or five more all together, and they were away with a splendid wild crash of music, all close together with no doubt or hesitation, sweeping away in a tight white line, noses down, running fast.

Kirk stood entranced for a moment, but already the followers were toiling up to that far-away crest, taking different lines, all of them steep the moment they left the water. Out to the right there was the long-legged huntsman with four of the terriers. Running along the flat Kirk came up behind him; but Gerallt went so fast with his long legs and his ceaseless springing stride that Kirk could stay with him only by putting all his closest attention to it, taking advantage of every easy step, watching the huntsman's feet in front and above, concentrating all the time. The least stumble jerked the breath out of him, losing distance; sometimes he was on all fours; often he seized the grass with his nearer hand to help him along, always too far behind to relax his concentration for a moment. He saw almost nothing of the hounds as they hunted up and along the side and over the rim at the very nick in the rock where the fox had stood, but all the time there was that lovely remote barbarous din to keep him tearing along like a boy. He meant to keep with Gerallt if he possibly could, both as an expert fox-hunter and as his only acquaintance – the Master was too awful a figure by far – and already there was a tacit understanding between them: most of the followers hunted in pairs.

Kirk saw the top of the ridge coming at last, and he fairly ran up the last stretch. Gerallt was already there, gazing down at the great sweep of country the other side.

Below them stretched a tumult of rounded hills, a heaving ocean of rock frozen and set aeons ago. From high above, from this Craig Llyn Du where they stood, the roundness was strikingly apparent, although from below nothing of it could be seen. The lower hills sloped down to the shining face of Llyn Cidwm far in the distance – Llyn Cidwm he knew – and beyond the water the mountains rose dimly, merging into the general grey of a dull overcast sky, cold, with rain threatening and the worse threat of low cloud: already the bare head of Moel y Gigfran had wisps passing over it.

Most of the other followers were on the ridge. The woman magistrate's hair straggled somewhat, but on the whole they all looked surprisingly composed. 'They must have hearts like steam-engines,' reflected Kirk, privately feeling his own.

There was no sign of the hounds. Once the distant clamour of the sheepdogs of Rhaiadr Mawr made all heads turn, and once a movement of sheep far below half deceived them: then the Master spoke briefly to Gerallt and they began to move down towards a jutting crag that would command the ground directly beneath them – a wide tract that was invisible from the ridge of Llyn Du. From here they saw a man far below, a small dark figure pointing away towards the lake with repeated emphatic jerks of his stick.

'He's gone for Moel y Gigfran,' said Gerallt, in a voice between statement and question: the Master nodded, and they turned northward, keeping along a high broad undulating ridge with outcropping pillars of granite. Presently the followers were scattered over a furlong or two, with Gerallt and Kirk somewhat ahead, taking the higher ground. They were not going so fast now by any means, and Gerallt told Kirk about a noson lawen where he had sung penillion all last night to Maire Votty's harp. 'Up until three I was, and home by the light of the moon, four miles over the old mountain.' He sang one or two of the penillion, and a stanza from *Timotheus cried*. Kirk had loosened up now; his second wind had come, and as he swung along over the close turf he felt a great well-being – he could go on for ever – he would be in at the kill! They went up and down, up and down, but there was nothing steep, and Gerallt was not pressing himself.

Now there was a distinct cry of hounds before them, and every face lightened: it was clear they were in the right road. Then from a knoll Gerallt saw them and pointed them out, a line of long white dots, like sheep, but moving fast and continuously. The wind was increasing now, blowing from behind them, snatching the noise of the hounds from their ears; but when the wind slackened, or when they were under

a lee, they could hear it plain – clearly the hounds were
quite near their fox, pushing him along handsomely.

At a given point the Master came to a halt, with the
followers ranged at various distances from him; and they
all gazed up at the massive side of the Moel y Gigfran. It
seemed a terribly long way off to Kirk, and he could hardly
distinguish the hounds at all by the time they ran over the
ridge, over the back of the bald mountain, away from the
lake. There was some talk about the line the fox would take
– a flood of place-names, for every rock, pass, pool or bothie
had its name – and presently Gerallt started away again,
bearing left-handed: the Master and most of the others
stayed in the shelter of the crag, a few more in a dell below,
and Kirk hesitated, unwilling to attach himself to the
huntsman too obviously – to appear to cling. A few minutes
later the tall soldier, followed by the schoolmaster and the
virgin, struck directly up towards the top of the mountain,
while another group went away diagonally for the ridge.
Gerallt was already a small active form, moving through
the heather in the middle distance. The Master sat down
and lighted his pipe. Kirk stood irresolutely a little longer
and then dropped down from the crag in the same direction
as Gerallt.

Soon he was out of sight of all the rest, both before and
behind. To his right he had the high irregular side of the
mountain and to his left the valley, with the road far below
and the lake: he was going along a rough, boulder-strewn
plain, a great step or terrace half-way up the side of the
Moel.

Presently it seemed to him that he had been on his own a
long while, with nothing but the wind and the emptiness
around him – too long, and he was increasingly afraid that
he would never be with the hounds again. It was a world
given over to the raven: a pair of them passed high over it,
communicating through three miles of air, steadily croaking
one to the other. He might have been alone in it – no sign

of men at all – for although he caught distant glimpses of the road it was so remote that it belonged to another planet entirely, another life. The ground, which had been reasonably plain in the distance, now proved to be full of bogs, some standing in defiance of nature on the slope, and with rocky clefts that needed care and circumspection – pitiably slow. It called for a great deal of effort too, and in time it warmed him finely in spite of the searching wind: he was wiping sweat from his face when he saw Gerallt far up on his right, much higher than he had expected and farther away than he had supposed possible. It was heartening to see him at all however, and Kirk turned directly up the main slope. The lie of the land was now such that the valley, the sweeping great valley Nant Cidwm, was shut out of his view, and only the rising hulk of the mountain with the racing drifts of cloud on it remained to show him the way.

The stimulus of the sight of Gerallt died after he had gone another cruel hard mile, and on the top of a viewpoint that showed him nothing but a thousand acres of desolation and the dislocated skeleton of a sheep he stopped to take breath and to consider. There were so many ways they could have gone without his seeing them, and the likelihood of his being still in the right direction was very small. For the last long stretch he had been working round the side of Moel y Gigfran, climbing and turning among rocky gullies, going where he could rather than where he would, and now he was by no means sure which way round he was. The mountain seemed to rise in both directions, and he stood there in a state of tired despondency, undecided and wet-foot, with disappointment welling up.

He stood long enough for the cold to get at him, so that he was glad to be moving again. But he went heavily now, with no spirit, and his sad mind had already returned to the prosaic road so far below and how he should reach it and the paper-work that would be waiting for him at the weary end when he came round a shoulder of the mountain and saw the hounds and the followers not two hundred yards ahead.

They were grouped among a tumbled mass of boulders in a sloping waste of shale – the backside of the Moel – and the hounds were lying here and there upon the rocks, licking their paws or staring vacantly. Kirk's face creased with instant joy: his heart beat double-time. He walked up, looking as unconcerned as he could manage.

This was the Ddear Felin, an ancient fox and badger stronghold; and in the middle of the boulders he could see the bowed back of the Master, head and shoulders down a cleft between two yellow rocks. Gerallt's head was also down the hole, his body arched over the Master's: they were listening intently. Major Boyd sat by the earth, holding a tight mob of terriers: an empty couple showed that some of them had already been put to. One thin black-and-tan bitch barked unceasingly and every now and then all the others would join in, screaming and bawling. When they were not pulling, reared on their hind legs, they sat trembling all over, whining shrill. Boyd's temper had improved with his walk; he told Kirk that they had run their fox in, that Bellman had marked him true for quite half an hour, and that it would be the Devil's own job to bolt him. He suggested that Kirk should post himself on that tall rock down there to view him away, if the terriers could make him budge.

The boulder was rough and harsh – a pleasure to creep up after all the treacherous wet slate of the other side – and from its flat top Kirk surveyed the whole of the earth, a mass of loose rock ten yards across and running twenty down the slope; some of the boulders that formed it were as big as a cart, but most were smaller; and many of these had obviously been moved before – they showed raw yellow underneath. Above the earth shale ran up clear for three or four hundred feet: below, the slope was less, and there was some grass and heather among the rocks. On the far side from Kirk, the way he had come, there was the shoulder of the mountain, and it broke the full force of the wind: behind him still more shale stretched away, its lower edge ending in much the same kind of grass, heather and bog, scattered with boulders fallen from the high crags of the Moel y Gigfran. Above the shale nothing but bare rock, vague in the thickening cloud.

Other followers were posted here and there on vantage-points, and Kirk saw with satisfaction that there were not so many now as there had been. In the lee of a crag the women were mending a torn skirt with safety-pins. Clearly it was his duty to watch the broken ground below him, a gully whose nearer end was hidden from the rest, and for the first quarter of an hour he stared eagerly, rarely taking his eyes off to see what they were doing at the earth. Then his nearest neighbour began to eat his lunch – a turkey's leg with crusty bread. The sight brought an instant, painful salivation, a grind in his stomach, and Kirk realized that he was shockingly hungry. Cautiously he dragged his sand-wiches from an inner pocket, still keeping his eye on the gully; but what with the business of separating the wet conglomerate and of keeping insistent hounds from eating the pieces before he could get them to his mouth – gently insistent hounds, but tall and pervasive – his very close attention dwindled. He engulfed the food, a wretched pittance, mostly bread with cake-crumbs ground into it from his repeated falls; and by the time it was gone all the warmth he had generated on his way up had left him. Now the wind was a continual enemy; no crouching or huddling would escape it, and soon it pierced even into his protected middle parts. His eyes watered as he stared at the gully; his hands, reaching for his pipe, were too numb to do more than fumble impotently at the buttons; his neck and shoulders were rigid with shivering. He looked enviously at Gerallt and the Master, now shifting masses of rock, scarlet with exertion. They had changed terriers – the magistrate had charge of the disgraced muddy couple – but still the little dogs were not doing very much: all cry and no wool. A Jack Russell kept skipping about on the top, searching and searching for a new entry – she thought nothing of the place where the others were, four or five of them who kept up a muffled bawling and scuffling deep underground. Kirk watched her with an apathetic stare: he had never been so cold in his life.

The present seemed always with him, and this vile wind. The man on the far side seemed to be suffering even more, cupping his frozen ears with an unconscious look of pure misery.

The Jack Russell was screaming away, bouncing over the rocks with desperate energy, yelping at every bound: nothing of this pierced Kirk's numbed mind for two beats of time, then everything was movement – hounds streaming down and round the far shoulder, the men all standing, bolt upright and motionless, the Master shouting to the highest of them all, incomprehensible words in the wind – and he realized that the fox had stolen away, had crept an unbelievable distance from the earth before breaking, and although he had passed close by two or three hounds only the terrier had seen him.

One of the farmers was already racing up the crag at the corner of the shale: at the top he paused and pointed, with a shout flung back over his shoulder. A moment later the hounds swung right-handed, all giving tongue, and they came back into view. Kirk stared ahead of them, searching the heather for the fox. To his intense surprise he found himself hoping that the fox was well ahead – that it should at least have a fair run for its life. Indeed, that it should get away.

The whole pack crossed on the flat ground three hundred yards below, and behind them the white terrier, yelling still. The whole pack in deadly earnest: there was not a hound but spoke, and the music echoed from the Moel behind and a ragged cliff in front, echoed and reverberated, though torn by the wind. Its beauty had a devilish, pitiless quality, thought Kirk; yet when the hounds checked at a bog over to the right and fell almost silent, his excitement faded; and when almost immediately afterwards they hit off the line again with a splendid crash, he felt a wild exultation.

It looked as though the fox were making for a small earth farther along at the bottom of the shale, but they were pressing him too hard and he ran on past it, on and round. They were running so fast that they were out of sight in a few minutes; and presently they were out of hearing too, the wind being foul.

The followers waited to see whether he would turn left-handed again into the high broken country behind the Moel, and Kirk took the chance to peer into the earth. He could see nothing but tumbled rock with here and there a brown shrivel of small fern or a handful of crude harsh red earth. It seemed quite impossible that a fox should have got away so far without having been seen.

There were still two terriers down, and Gerallt stayed to bring them out. Major Boyd started up the shale in a sloping line for the ridge: another group went along the bottom in the direction the fox had taken. The Master watched them go, then turned back the way Kirk had come: as he left he spoke to Gerallt – a word over his shoulder, torn away by the wind. Gerallt understood it, however, and laughed.

When they were alone Gerallt asked Kirk to hold the remaining terriers, and bent to the earth. Without looking up he said, 'So you came along then, Doctor?'

'That's right,' said Kirk.

The terriers were wedging one another far down under the rocks; they could be heard quarrelling, and nothing Gerallt could do would bring them up. Eventually he and Kirk and the other dogs walked away from the earth altogether: two minutes later the terriers came out, matted and entirely changed in colour.

They set out after the Master, and now Kirk was glad that Gerallt was going fast; in a little while warmth flooded through him, reanimating all but his hands and ears, and he could enjoy being alive once more. They were going directly away from the obvious line, but it was clear that if the fox carried right round the top of the Moel this course would bring them out charmingly.

Once they were round the shoulder they caught the full force of the wind, colder now by far, and the first handful of rain came driving flat along it. Kirk and Gerallt turned up their collars at almost the same moment: it was not much of a protection, to be sure, but they treasured that two inches of dry neck.

It was a long while before they saw the Master again. He was walking rapidly up a distant slope, away from them and below, strangely foreshortened. He and they were going in almost exactly the same direction. 'Surely,' thought Kirk, 'this is a good sign.' For now to him *good* once more meant being with the hounds, hunting the fox and eventually killing him.

Ever since they had come round into the wind they had been travelling diagonally towards the Cidwm valley: hard going all the way, and Kirk had to put so much physical and spiritual energy into keeping up with the huntsman that he had little time to inspect his own attitude towards the fox, towards the fox's fate. Once on an even slope he made an observation about 'wanting to have his cake and to eat it'; and another time, when Gerallt was untangling the terriers, he recalled the same ambivalence at a bull-fight – his pleasure when the goaded bull hurled a torero into the crowd: but no more than that.

The mountainside stretched away behind them, and now they were looking down again into Nant Cidwm, with the lake almost behind them. They must be in the next county by now, thought Kirk, glancing at his watch. It had stopped,

however; stopped hours or miles ago, some unremembered
fall having sprung its works.

The Master was sitting under the lee of a rock with his
black dog, watching his hounds work along a dry ravine.
The scent was poor down there, the day growing so precious
cold, but they were working it out cleverly, all close together,
with their noses down and their bottoms wriggling eagerly.
After a while the Master said that young Lucifer was shaping
well – he might be quite a good dog yet. They carried the
line right across, and at the far edge of the ravine they
started running again, a hound with a deep mouth speaking
all the time. Still they bore away right-handed, and it
seemed that the fox was running a true ring, a great elliptical
path with the Moel as its centre, irregular in places but
always tending back to its beginning.

They walked now on the inside of this ring, keeping the
hounds in view for a good while. Since they were on the
higher ground, they could see the hunting of the pack to
perfection, and Kirk was so taken up with doing this and
with remaining upright that by the time the hounds ran
clean away he no longer had the least notion of where he was
– from this high table-land he could see not a single familiar
shape: north and south were buried in the clouds.

Some time after the pack had disappeared the three men
sat down on a knoll: now and then they heard the dogs,
and sometimes, from the movement of sheep, they could tell
where they were. Kirk could not make out why they sat
there, why they did not go on after the hounds; but he was
happy to sit, and what strength his mind still possessed was
taken up with thoughts of food.

A quarter of an hour later they were going along at a
great pace, pushing in a straight determined line across the
country: the reasons for this move were utterly obscure –
Kirk thought he must have dozed momentarily in spite of
the cold, because he had suddenly started up to the sound
of urgent Welsh, and then immediately afterwards they had

set off. 'Without sleep, there is no waking,' he said, nodding to himself. 'That's logic.'

Time passed, and his hunger with it. From time to time as they traversed this stony wilderness they paused to listen, and it seemed to Kirk that they were anxious now. At last, far ahead, they heard a hound, a single deep bell-like voice. They stopped to make certain, for the wind had often made a noise like baying as it eddied in the higher crags; and indeed there it was, clear and certain, directly forward.

'It's marking in the Ceunant he is,' said Gerallt: or rather he put out the words as a suggestion. The Master waited a moment longer and then nodded. They went on faster still and presently four or five hounds met them, young hounds, capering idly about. The pack had run their fox to earth; they had grown tired of waiting and they were scattering abroad. Unless the marking hound stayed where he was, the fox was lost.

Gerallt called them in and ran forward, bounding like an enormous hare and bawling 'Yo mark her then, Countess. Yo mark her then, Ranter. Ooick, Ranter, yo mark to him, boy.'

Some of the hounds that had broken back began hunting away to the right on a frivolous line and now the Master's voice joined in as he lifted them off it. 'Aah, you bloody rebels. Lucifer, Lucifer, you bloody sod. God damn and blast that bloody Lucifer.'

Kirk heard the twanging of the horn as he toiled up the slope, and all at once there he was on the edge of the Ceunant, an abrupt, unexpected cleft, a narrow gorge, a shale and grass slope running down to jagged rocks and a white stream far below: it wanted only a few more vertical degrees to be a precipice. Gerallt was already far down its face, scrambling and sliding at a breakneck rate, still roaring like a bull. He was making for an outcrop of grey rock that jutted from the slope, with three good hounds below it, marking still – Ringwood, Countess and Ranter.

Half consciously Kirk noticed the care with which the hound in front of him launched itself over the edge: nothing much, but a horribly significant little check that made him feel sick as he too went over. It was worse than he had thought, the farthest limit of what two feet could manage; but his stick, his nailed boots and two or three providential rocks kept him from plummeting headlong to the distant stream, and with a last wild rush he reached the outcrop. Here, with the flat top firm under his feet, he found that his body was trembling all over – that the height had made him so dizzy he could hardly stand.

The Master was there immediately after him; without a pause he passed his terriers to Kirk and slipped down to join Gerallt below. A double note of the horn brought the stragglers racing in from the far side, and now the terriers were put to. The earth was a long cleft in the base of the rock, a cleft that ran up until it became a hair-like crack. The terriers below were madly excited; they set up the wildest bawling, and before he was aware the little brutes that Kirk was holding hurled themselves at the edge and very nearly had him over. He braced himself against their pull, squatting on the rock, and he yelled at them; but they took no notice of his voice, nor of his stick, though he rapped them hard.

From this position he could see nothing: he did not mind that at all however – the near prospect of being plucked over that edge had quite daunted him. The sheer twenty feet and the plunging slope below had woken all his latent vertigo: his stomach heaved: the landscape turned.

Presently he heard Gerallt's voice calling him. The terriers, who had grown resigned, instantly redoubled their fury, heaving him towards the break. He thumped them brutally and edged to a place from which he could see the huntsman.

'Would you come down here just a minute, Doctor?' he asked.

'May I let the terriers go?'

'Oh no indeed. You must not let the terriers go, Doctor bach.'

It was a hellish experience. Where the rock met the shale was the only way down, and it was vertical – only a few widely-spaced and uncertain stones to give any footing at all. Without the right use of his hands and with the terriers liable to hurl him off his balance at any moment, it seemed impossible. However, this time his low, savage, earnest cursing impressed the dogs: he dangling them ruthlessly by their collars, dragged them over rock; and, gravity and good luck helping, it was done. He came into the comparative safety of the slope under the outcrop: Gerallt handed him those terriers that were not already underground and recommended his going back to the top, as the best place for watching for the fox to bolt. Kirk faced the return with a kind of desperation; in fact it was far easier than the descent. The terriers pulled eagerly, and he clawed up after them.

With all these dogs milling about it was hard to find a firm place to sit: but with brutal dragooning he did clear a good recess, a recess with a grip for his heels, some way back from the hideous edge; and there he sat. He could not tell what was happening below without peering over – an impossibility until this vertigo could be mastered – so there he stayed, feeling his bruises, reflecting upon giddiness and its unreasonable panic, and staring vacantly at the terriers until the Master's voice called for more by name. Kirk did not know any of their names, but he slipped those who seemed most eager to go. He seemed to have done right, for there was no sound of reproach, and some minutes later the Master called for another couple, adding 'That Tory had a grip on him now'. Kirk was left with the two quietest: old bald-faced bitches with few teeth between them, who had been brought only because it broke their hearts to be left.

He felt the dizziness recede, and the illogical dread; and

to test the effect of height again he stood up. He had taken two paces towards the edge when he saw the fox on the shale twenty yards below the earth, running hard and fast in a bunched-up long-legged gallop, its tail held up in a curve.

Instantly he bawled 'Gone away', and there again was the Jack Russell with another terrier by her, flying over the rocks. But every hound had been idling on the far side, and although they were laid on with might and main they were slow away, and with intense relief Kirk saw the fox racing between the boulders right down towards the stream before they began to run on his line.

This time the terriers were all out directly, all but one, and they did not wait for him. The fox had run straight up the Ceunant for a quarter of a mile, then up the side where it was very bare and rocky, and so over the ridge behind. They talked a little as they followed – the atmosphere was different, now that there were only the three of them left – and the Master said that until this last minute he had supposed they had changed foxes, had put up a fresh fox by Llys Dafydd; but now he saw that it was the same. Gerallt said that Countess had marked very well, and the Master agreed – she was a nice little bitch.

The wind met them again at the top of the ridge with even greater force: they saw hounds on the other side of the valley, working slowly up the far slope: far more slowly now.

'It's this damned cold wind spoiling the scent,' said the Master.

They went down, across the marshy bottom and up the other side. Up and up the other side: it seemed unending, and the muscles on the front of Kirk's thighs hurt so much that he thought they must refuse their duty. He poled himself up with his stick, working out each step ahead: and there was the top, the strain gone as though he had dropped a heavy load. He paused a moment to look at his meaningless watch and breathe deep, staring round the grey, indeterminate landscape. The others were twenty yards ahead now, and he broke into a shambling run to catch up. Down the hill, then up another. How he wished they would stop, if only for a minute. To sit in the shelter of a rock long enough to smoke a small pipe out . . .

How interminably the upward slope climbed on! How he hated the steadily marching backs in front of him. Now a wall, a stone wall with a strand of old barbed wire on top of it; and the terriers had to be helped over. Kirk went last, and by the time he had leapt down, jarring every fibre of his being, the others were well beyond it, going fast. Again the stumbling run, the trip and fall, before he joined them.

Another wall – this mountainside was checkered with them, great unsteady dry-stone barriers – another slope. But at least this slope was down and for a few hundred yards it changed the strain, until the long fore-reaching jolt made a climb almost welcome again. Now the hounds were at a check in the wet dead ground at the bottom and the men paused to let them work. With Bellman and Ranter and the cleverer hounds leading they cast round and about on the far side, but it was some time before they could hit off the line again. Kirk was happy to see the others sit on stones as willingly as he did himself and show evident signs of fatigue: he had begun to think them immortal. As the ghost-like hounds wafted to and fro he felt a hint of strength coming back into his legs: he might, if pushed, manage to get up again. Now Ranter hit the line; Countess owned it too, and some other hounds; and although they were no longer speaking with that old passionate conviction, they ran straight, all together, and up the other side.

It was not until he was half-way up the next slope, climbing a wall again, that Kirk recognized the familiarity of the darkening countryside. They were mounting towards the Craig Llyn Du, going painfully up the way they had come down so very long ago. Here the scent was patchy; the hounds had to puzzle out the line almost yard by yard, and now they hardly spoke at all. Slowly they carried it up and up, right to the great curtain of rock; and as their white forms zigzagged up the steepest part Kirk fell behind. His lungs and heart seemed to be bursting, and although he was climbing still it was only because of a check that he was able to come up with them. Up up and beyond to the edge of the bitterly cold lake from which the water fell so far to Llyn Du. Up here the ice was forming, and the crust tinkled underfoot.

From the high lake the hounds came back along the stream to the falls, and now it seemed that they had certainly lost their fox. It took them twenty minutes to work over the bare rock in the howling wind, but at last Countess, casting ahead as far as the heather, spoke on the true strong line – the fox must be failing, his scent growing fatally strong – and the others came to her. They ran fast down the length of the fall, checked for a short while at the bottom and then while the men sat and watched them they ran with a fine cry along the shores of Llyn Du and over the lower edge of the valley that enclosed the lake, down to the broken country out of sight.

They must be very near him, thought Kirk as they began to go down. Down, from rock to rock with here and there a patch of heather; they dropped fast, ten times faster than the weary road up, and when they reached the bottom Kirk reflected that he might as well have stayed below all the time. More usefully too, for then he could have gone along to see which way they had taken in the difficult country beyond: his heavy mind was obstinately fixed on the notion of the chase.

They splashed along – it was marshy here – and both the Master and Gerallt were listening – they were uneasy – the hounds had fallen mute too suddenly. Had they run into their fox? He was sure they had not.

The lake was far longer this time; there were waves on it and a yellow foam on the leeward shore. It took a long time to reach the place where the sloping ground began; and there they were met by several hounds coming slowly back, quite at a loss and dispirited. No sound of any marking, and indeed Ranter, the most steadfast hound in the pack, joined them a moment later, with Countess and Bellman. It was clear that the unceasing bitter wind had been too much at last – the failing scent would not lie; and when they came to a little ravine with a path running through it the Master said, 'Well, I think I shall go home now, Doctor. Where did you leave your car?'

'At the end of the road,' said Kirk. He was standing with his back to the wind, facing one of the many sudden up-thrusts of rock that lined the hillside: on the face of it, seven or eight feet up, were three ledges, two bare and one with heather growing. On the heather-covered ledge there lay the fox. Dead-beat, wet, matted, flattened. Kirk closed his mouth suddenly with an audible intake of breath: he peered furtively at the Master's tired, drawn face and turned away from the ledge in case it should be obvious where he was looking. The Master bent to his horn and blew a lovely note, long and true; then another: the fox did not stir.

At last they were moving down the path, the huntsman in front, then a long string of hounds with more joining them from either side, then a bunch of sober terriers, many of them carrying a leg, then the Master with his old black dog moving stiffly, then Kirk; they went down the rocky defile with their heads bowed against the wind, down to the long road home.

On the Bog

———◆◆◆———

'IT IS TIME to be moving,' said Boyle.

'What? What?' cried Meagher, starting wildly out of his sleep – a cry of alarm.

Boyle made no reply, but flashed his lighter to look for the leg of the tall thigh-boots beside him; indeed there was no need for a reply, since the momentary gleam showed the whole scene at once, the interior of a reed-walled butt, guns, a game-bag, duck-boarded floor, the wooden bench. The flame also lit Boyle's handsome face, exaggerating its high arrogant nose and the morning beard; and in this brief flash Meagher's being fell back into its present context.

They had lain out on the bog all night, so that they could get out to the far end for the geese, for the dawn-flighting, well before daybreak and well before any keepers were moving.

Of course it had been Boyle's idea entirely. In Jammet's a man was prating about geese, great skeins of greylags brought down by the hard weather, and turning to Meagher Boyle said 'How should you like to have a shot in the morning? I know a capital place, and you are the great wildfowler, I believe.'

Meagher was pleased, flattered with the notice and the preference – particularly the preference, because toad-eating Clancy was there, eager for any invitation that might be going; and although he had been up at a party all night before he said he would be very happy indeed – 'wildfowling is meat and drink to me'. They left at once, walked over the river to Boyle's place – Meagher was one of the few who had been there – and loaded gun-cases, cartridge-bags and tarpaulin into the car.

'It is the devil we have no dog,' said Boyle. 'Clancy spoke of a labrador.'

'Oh, that was only his froth and pride; he has never owned so much as a cat in all his life. I'll act as the dog,' said Meagher, laughing.

Boyle sent him for cartridges with a five-pound note and as soon as he came back they drove straight out of the town. A long drive, too fast for conversation with the hood off, fast along winding lanes and boreens, and Meagher was excited with the rushing air, pleased to be sitting there next to Boyle: then the stop in the lee of a turf-stack and the walk out, a great way across rough pasture as far as a dyke. 'We are not going in there, are we?' asked Meagher, reading a notice in the fading light. It was one of many posted all along the near bank forbidding trespassers, warning of mantraps, stating that dogs should be shot on sight.

'That is the general idea,' said Boyle. He felt for a plank in the rushes, laid it across, lifted the wire the far side, slipped through and stood waiting.

'I don't mind a bit of poaching,' said Meagher, 'but . . .' He could not find an acceptable way of putting 'but only when it is fairly safe', so he said no more. This was certainly far from safe: he did not know which county they were in even, but they had run along two miles of park wall with an enormous house inside it just before stopping, and now they stood in flat open country without a bush or a hedge for miles. The notices were fresh and trim; this was obviously a strictly preserved estate.

'Never worry about them,' said Boyle. 'You are only an honorary dog; and in any case geese and duck are not game. They are ferae naturae – they have no animus revertendi.'

Meagher could hardly reply to that. He walked on over the tussocky forbidden ground, looking as unconscious and confident as he could. They had not gone a hundred yards before a single partridge got up in front of them, a little to the right. Boley's gun leapt to his shoulder; he fired, and the bird hit the ground so hard it bounced twice. He said, 'I beg pardon, Meagher. That was really your bird. Just pick it up, will you, there's a good fellow.'

Meagher picked it up, glancing round in every direction; and he picked up two rabbits and a snipe as well before they reached downright bog with redshanks in the cuttings and curlews crying high overhead. Looking ahead in the twilight he could see tall reeds, dense cover that would hide their nakedness; but between them and the reeds lay an intricate series of channels, many of them newly dredged. Boyle led the way through, walking casual and easy like a tenant for life and a man who knows his way well.

'You seem to know your way well,' said Meagher.

'I used to come here in the old duke's time,' said Boyle. And some time later, pushing through the innermost reeds, he said, 'The old boy always did himself proud. Just look at this butt, will you? Now that's what I call a truly ducal butt. Benches, duck-boarding. There will be straw in that barrel; but suppose you cut some rushes as well – here is a knife. I will keep an eye lifted in case the duck start to move.'

Meagher could have sworn he had not slept at all that night. Certainly with his prickling eyes and general weariness he felt he had not. The greater part of it (all but the last twenty minutes in fact) he had lain listening to Boyle snoring on his back, listening to the desolate call of marsh-birds he could not put a name to, weird shrieks and groanings, and to the stir of the reeds as ice formed on them. He was not very cold as he lay there in his nest of rushes and straw under a piece of tarpaulin, but he was wet from below and hungry, and as the hours wore by he smoked until he had no more in his packet. He was a heavy smoker, deeply addicted to cigarettes.

It was partly anger that kept him awake, anger and resentment. They had not been in the butt half an hour before the duck began flighting, mallard, wigeon, teal, pintail, great numbers of them, and Boyle set up a fusillade, a firework display, an artillery battle, that must have been heard five miles off at least in this deathly calm air. Every shot made Meagher wretched, and by the time the movement was over and he had searched out a good score of birds he was in such a state of nervous indignation that he almost cried out, 'You invite me to shoot and without a word of warning to expose me to this sort of thing – you have no consideration at all.'

The only words that actually passed were Boyle's. He said, 'I think it is over: in any case it is too dark to see. I cannot wait to get at the geese. Good night to you, now.' No jocular or commiserating reference to the few ineffectual half-hearted shots that Meagher had let off: tact, that was the lay, a tact so obvious that it was, if not a studied offence, then at least most unfriendly.

Their acquaintance ran back a considerable way, so far that Meagher could say of Boyle, 'We are old friends: I have known him for years,' but it had never really matured: there was too little in the way of candid interchange, too much reserve for that. Meagher admired Boyle's undeniable style, his offhand way with people, and his occasional lavish generosity; but he had few illusions; he knew that Boyle liked to have a companion – he had no girl, no permanent judy, preferring temporary drabs of the lowest kind – and as Meagher was generally available so he was the most frequently chosen. Then again he knew that although Boyle could talk freely about Stockhausen, Schwitters, Brecht, he was virtually illiterate: none of the things that interested Meagher concerned Boyle in the least: he would

see the National Library, the Gallery and the Abbey go up
in flames with cheerful indifference. Occasionally a wild,
unpredictable gaiety would come over him and then he
would lay aside his reserve, horsing around in Mother Daly's
like a boy; but on the whole he was elusive – there was no
coming close to him at all – and rather than friendship
between them there was a kind of exasperated love on
Meagher's side alone, a love not only for Boyle's thorough-
bred grace, his elegance, his ability to cope with guns, rods,
horses, waiters and girls, but also for his vulnerability.
Boyle was a man who had to be on top: he had to excel in
every field. Humiliation would destroy him – if a girl were
to turn him down or if he were to scrape a bus as he shot
his car one-handed through the whirlpool of College Green
he would be undone. In some fields – in talk – Meagher
could protect him; and to protect such a creature was a
privilege, an infinite superiority. Boyle walked a perpetual
tightrope, and although up until now he had never stumbled
badly to Meagher's knowledge he was continually in danger
of doing so, in danger deliberately created by himself. Blazing
away as though he owned creation on preserved land stuffed
with keepers: a perfect example.

As though he owned creation . . . he must own quite a
share of it, however. How much nobody knew, but certainly
more than most of their circle, certainly very much more
than Meagher, who lived by expedients – small journalism,
a little reviewing, the occasional grant. Once he had taken
Meagher and a couple of dreadful little bus-stop tarts to a
house behind Enniskerry, letting himself in with his key:
half had been ruined so long ago that trees grew twenty feet
out of it, but the rest was deeply comfortable, though dusty
– carpets, huge leather chairs, mahogany – and the drive
was kept up. He also had a tower in the County Clare,
where he fished: but many of them claimed to have towers
in the County Clare and what really impressed them was
this visible car, the sight of him coming out of the Kildare

Street Club, and his beautiful cigarette-case, made of gold. The car might be uninsured, the tower a myth, but the case was there all the time.

Money: that was the great trouble. When they went out, who picked up the restaurant bill? Who paid for the drinks, the petrol, the tickets? Usually Boyle was delicate, but he had a sadistic streak in him and sometimes he could make Meagher feel all the difference between a man with fifty pounds in his pocket and one with a packet of pawn-tickets done up with an elastic band. There were times when instead of offering a lift, a dinner-jacket, a loan, he would compel Meagher to make the direct request; once or twice he had casually borrowed one of Meagher's precious pounds and had forgotten to repay. Odd little meannesses too, such as disappearing for a moment and coming back with a freshly-lit cigarette. No doubt they arose from a dislike of being sponged on, of being manipulated; and fellows like Clancy were shameless at sponging.

Yet in spite of all this they laughed at many of the same things; they enjoyed the same films; they could be companionable enough; they had fun; and surely, said Meagher, fundamentally Boyle had a liking for him, and respected his parts.

The liking was not apparent on either side at this moment, however. Something seemed to have happened to their relationship during the night, as though Meagher's resentment and silent injurious expressions had conveyed themselves into the other's sleeping mind; or as though Boyle had reflected upon Meagher's 'I do not mind poaching but . . .' and had filled in the gap, or upon his ignominious performance with the gun (Meagher was a countryman only by theory). While for his part Meagher could not see why he made all this coil about a mere dilettante, a sciolist, a dabbler. 'I am far more intelligent than he is, far better educated,' he reflected, plucking straw and rushes from his

clothes. 'He may have a bodily, an animal intelligence – he
is good at killing things – but surely to God a man is above
a brute. He has read nothing at all.'

Here Boyle finished buckling his thigh-boots and walked
out of the butt, leaving the game-bag for Meagher to carry:
in the reeds outside he lit a cigarette, and at the smell of
the returning waft Meagher's stomach gave an avid craving
heave. He remembered not only that his packet was empty
but that he had had neither dinner nor tea. To be sure,
Boyle had eaten nothing either; but Boyle was well padded,
whereas Meagher, who lived by his wits, was painfully thin.
The gap of a meal told on him at once.

'Perhaps that is why I am feeling so very brittle all over,'
he thought. 'That and two sleepless nights. And I dare say
I have a cold coming on – to lie out all night in the wet,
what a notion! – a bad go of flu.'

He followed Boyle through the reeds: they walked without
speaking to one another, as though there were an acknowledged breach. Through the reeds round the lake and out
on the far side; and here, stretching infinitely far beyond
them, was the landscape of a dream, perfectly silent,
perfectly still; the whole bog, with every rush and clump of
grass upon it, was white with hoar-frost, and it gleamed
gently in a suffused shadowless light that came dropping
from the frozen air together with minute crystals of ice: no
visible source for the light, no stars, no moon, only this high
luminous mist. A world before the creation. An enormous
flatness with no details in it, for the impression of light was
illusory and at any distance everything merged into un-
certainty; there was no one object that could be seized and
defined apart from the sea-wall away to their left, the single
firm line in this universal vagueness, a line that ran curving
away for ever.

Boyle was screwing himself up to see his watch, to make
the hands show in the darkness of his bosom. 'Just hold my
gun, will you?' he said. A beautiful short-barrelled hammer-

less ejector, lighter by far than the old-fashioned brown keeper's gun allotted to Meagher.

'Can you make out the time?' asked Meagher, and to his shame he heard a placating note in his voice.

Boyle did not answer directly. In a cold impersonal tone he said, 'Only two hours to go. We shall have to step out if – oh for Christ's sake don't hold your gun like that, you silly whore! Don't you know you must never point your gun at anything you don't mean to kill?'

Meagher was on the edge of crying out that it was not pointed, that it was not loaded; but the shocking brutality of the assault, quite outside their habitual intercourse, choked back his lies and he followed Boyle in silence.

Two hours, he had said. Surely they had been walking more than two hours? The night seemed a hundred years old. The sea-wall was unchanged, the one firm thread in a shifting interminable dream; it stretched before and behind, a broad ten-foot earthwork with sluices here and there and every few hundred yards a set of posts, startlingly upright in a world so flat, like black exclamation marks signalling danger: each one might be an armed keeper. The idea of running away from a keeper, of labouring over the bog with a gun pointing at his back, was horrible to Meagher: and who could tell what Boyle might do, in such an encounter out here at the far end of the world with no one to see? He was a deeply bloody man. 'A whore, a pillar of ignorance,' said Meagher.

But although the sea-wall was still the same it no longer ran through the same country: now they had primaeval saltings on their left hand and the deep mud of a tidal river, while on the right the sweet-water marsh shone and glittered with creeping water. A landscape even more inhuman, desolate and unearthly than before: vaster too, for now an increase in the light had brought the indeterminate sea into its farther rim. The falling aerial crystals had turned to penetrating wet, but so far this had not affected the whiteness of the ground. The frost still struck upwards.

The mud seemed deeper underfoot, however – it had long since filled Meagher's inadequate shoes; and certainly his sick hunger and abject craving for tobacco had grown immeasurably. He felt even more brittle and his lack of sleep had got into his red-rimmed bleared watering eyes, so that when he concentrated on a post it flickered and even waved its arms; his sense of smell and his hearing had become unnaturally sharp. He heard the whistle of a flight of duck before Boyle, as they passed high overhead. These must be the first birds of the dawn-flighting; so surely the day could not be very far off, and release from this nightmarish entertainment?

Certainly there was more light, even if it was only the rising of the moon; but at the next set of posts this did not prevent him from catching his leg in the barbed wire slung between them. He gave a strong kick to be free of it: the wire broke from the post and snarled right round his leg, the barbs running deep. It nearly had him down: he staggered on one foot, his loaded gun swinging in an arc, pointing now at Boyle's head, now at his loins as he walked steadily on. Meagher recovered his balance, laid down the gun, laid down the game-bag (it weighed forty pounds), and knelt to wrestle with the wire. Wet with drizzle and mud, his numbed hands merely fumbled, and in a sudden flare of anger and resentment he tore at the wire with all his force. It was no good. He was still held fast, ignominiously kneeling there with the mud soaking into his knees; and in a sudden collapse of spirit he crouched against the post, watching Boyle stride away. He knew Boyle was aware – it was a conscious back – and he knew Boyle would not turn unless he were called upon for help.

Meagher did nothing until he saw the small leap of a flame: Boyle had lit a cigarette and was waiting for him. Meagher forced his mind to be cold, followed the pattern of the barbs and disentangled them one by one, tearing the cloth as he did so. He picked up the bag and followed, limping: as he got under way so the glow of the cigarette moved on.

Long before he caught up, the cord of the bag was biting into his shoulder again and the weight of the gun was a torment: he was wet through and through; he was full of yellow rancour and spleen; but with something of the cunning of fever he said 'I shall keep up with him: even Boyle has not the face to smoke without offering me one if I am right by him – a guest, for all love!'

He could feel the paper cylinder between his two fingers and his thumb, the glowing end sheltered in his palm from the drizzle, the deep inhalation, the yielding of the tube at the very end, the red arc and the hiss as he threw it into the water.

Still the old night faded and little by little the marsh came to life – heart-broken cries as dim birds fleeted away; rails grunting and squealing in a reed-bed; far over the devilish yell of a vixen. 'Do come along,' said Boyle once or twice. 'We shall never get there in time.'

A little while after they had passed a patch of black quaking bog with a dead bullock in the middle, its peeling horns and part of its head showing above the mud, a brace of teal sprung from a flash of water to the right of the wall, rising fast, almost vertically. Boyle missed them right and left. He walked on, saying nothing, faster than ever; and Meagher could tell from the set of his back that he was bitterly crossed.

'Do come on,' he said again, and now the light was spreading fast from the east, showing the white carcass of a boat on the far bank of the river. 'All I ask is a couple of shots at the geese. Just one pitiful shot; and we shall not get even that at this pace.'

On, faster still: Meagher did not give a damn in hell for the geese or the prospect of shooting at them, but Boyle's failure had revived his spirits a little and he walked along with his resentment somewhat appeased. Yet at the same time the sense of unreality – this unearthly landscape, his own light-headed fatigue – grew on him: his mind wandered off to other places and times, to odd, disconnected fantasies of triumph, and when he returned to the present he found he had dropped behind. He also found that his anger was dead: weary tolerance had replaced indignation.

Boyle had left the sea-wall some way before the point where it turned right-handed, and he was making his way cautiously through the mud towards a plank that led to a dense screen of reeds. Meagher did notice a soft gabbling in the distance, but it meant nothing to him. He only saw that by going straight along the wall he would avoid the mud and come to the bridge as soon as Boyle, thus making up for lost time. He did not catch Boyle's backward signal – the flash of his hand he would have used to a dog – and he hurried along with a sudden quick softening and a resolution to ask Boyle openly for a cigarette, to accept the humiliation of doing so, to gratify him. This was to be an offering, a reconciliation, and he called out 'Boyle, I say, Boyle.' As he called he saw the furious gesture and ducked; but it was too late. There was a monstrous threshing of wings on the far side of the reeds and the geese, hundreds, even thousands of geese, lifted high out of range.

As if he were alone Boyle walked on through the screen, taking no precautions now, and he went along the edge of the turlough where the smell of geese lay heavy, looking at the droppings and feathers: after some time he emerged, much farther round the bend, and came back along the wall. Meagher ran to meet him: his apologies died in his throat at the look, not of intense dislike or anger nor even fury but of utter contempt. A frigid, objective, dismissing contempt like a blow, breaking even the most rudimentary social contract. And while Meagher was uttering the few words he could force out, Boyle's eyes wandered off, bored, uninterested: he reached for his case, opened it – it gleamed like a chalice inside – deliberately chose and lit a cigarette.

Beside them, lower than the wall itself, a huge pale-blue bird came gliding through the frozen air, shadowless over the white ground, never moving its wings: behind and a little higher came its mate, even larger, dark and forbidding. They turned their heads to look at the men but they never deviated from their course; and as they flew a silence spread over the marsh – duck and small birds had been stirring; now they were mute. Not a sound, not a movement. Meagher's sense of the world was so altered that he saw them with no surprise: in this universe huge pale sinister birds might very well pass within handsreach.

Boyle's gaze followed them, and then as he turned to go he glanced at Meagher again, noticed that he was still speaking, moved his mouth into a civil, well-bred rictus, and walked off.

Meagher walked along behind him: the distress of this look, so much more fundamental than the rough words at their setting-out, combined with the unreality of the scene, with the monstrous birds, the silence, the unbelievable final severing of their relationship and with his own state of physical wretchedness to shake him so that he hardly knew what he was at.

He walked on a mile, close at heel, the general pain separating into its various components. Rage predominated, and the extreme of humiliation – ultimate humiliation: the rage made him tremble; it knotted his throat and his stomach. The expression on his very pale face was strange to him, like a mask imposed from outside. Yet he still thought he was indulging in fantasy when he said 'But it is you are the fool, Boyle, to go out no one knows where with a man you humiliate: it is you are the fool to put a gun in his hands and turn your back on him and walk where he can push you down into the slime for ever, you whore.' And even when he had the brown gun up and quivering behind Boyle's head it still seemed only unreal show and mime, part of the abiding nightmare all round; but his finger curled on the trigger and squeezed as he cried 'Like that!' and the gun shot out an orange flame.

The unexpected bang and the recoil quite stunned him: it was not until the slow smoke cleared that he saw Boyle in the water, motionless now. Meagher slid down the wall and stood up to his knees, straddling the body and bowed as though to heave it out. Blood flowed from the shattered head, pouring and turning like smoke in the water, and through the eddies rose an enormous eel.

Silence returned: only the raucous panting of his animal breath. Then from far away on the motionless air over the bog came a sound. He looked up – the sky had turned pale – but there was nothing above him. The sound grew stronger, a rhythmic singing beat, and turning his appalled staring face still higher he saw three swans. The first light of the sun touched them from below and they flashed pure against the blue, flying straight and fast from the north with their long necks stretched out before them. The rhythm changed a little, sighing and poignant: changed still more, and as they passed high overhead their wings sang in unison, bearing his spirit away and far, far away.

The Thermometer

THEY had nothing whatever to say to one another, and
between them the silence grew so massive that it could almost
be seen: on the one side of it a small boy – of what age?
Mr Carew had asked, but the reply had slipped his mind.
Below the age of puberty, no doubt, he reflected, taking the
short trousers as evidence, and by so much the more removed
from humanness: but how much below it? A squat and
meagre child. It might be anything. If it had been a specimen
– and it looked not unlike some of the swarthy things his
colleagues dissected – it would have had a label with all the
relevant information. What the devil could he do with it,
do with it? His mind trailed off into habitual repetition. Do
with it, do with it?

The boy saw a vast column of authority over against him,
omnipotent and grey. Grey the vague clothing that draped
the massive form, grey the enormous trousers, in grey folds
like the legs of an elephant; and the huge stone face,
expressionless and everlasting, was also grey. The boy was
not conscious of having stared, yet he knew that grey hair
not only covered that head, but also burst in tufts from the
ears, and even appeared, unnaturally straggling, on the
bridge of the nose. The only exception to this rule of grey
was the eyes, which were watery blue with red margins:
the boy did not look up, of course, but he was aware of
these eyes, gleaming weirdly through the thick, distorting
lenses of a pair of thin steel-rimmed spectacles, looking
across the silence at him – down at him, from a height of
about a yard above his own head and at a distance exactly
equal to the length of the piece of Turkey carpet on which

they stood. At the same time, but from different heights and distances, Koch, Pasteur, Ehrlich, Creighton, Beale and Muller, in frock-coats, beards and steel-rimmed spectacles, dignified, hairy, inhuman, gazed out from the walls into the middle of the room, adding to the silence.

The boy was oppressed by the silence, but not very much. He was not answerable for it; and so long as he stood still, without fidgeting, picking, staring, sniffing, gaping, biting his nails, stooping, gnawing the inside of his mouth or turning his toes in, he could not be blamed. At least, he could not be blamed by the rules; and he was willing to credit cousin Carew (for those enormous hair-backed hands which were now holding a watch on the blurred upward horizon of his field of vision belonged in fact to his paternal grandfather's nephew) with decency enough to observe the rules, if only at first. Being not to blame, therefore, he was free to argue out the pattern of the carpet and to absorb the various smells of the room – tobacco, books (the room was lined with them below a certain height and their backs gave off an odour of glue, dye and buckram: new books and shiny quarterlies), warmed town air, and above all chemicals, pungent and unfamiliar.

At one time during the silence Mr Carew had taken his watch out of his waistcoat pocket with an indistinct notion of holding it to his cousin's ear; but a moment's reflection had told him that this gesture would be quite unsuitable in the present case and he was in the act of closing it when his mind strayed off to its repetition of do with it, do with it, and from that point to a less uneasy general meditation, if not to a temporary mental stagnation.

The watch remained open in his hand: it was a hunter, and its outer cover stood at right angles from the dial, while between the two the leaf-thin inner cover caught the light in a double gleam. The whole looked like an exotic flower: the boy watched it with his eyes deliberately unfocused and somewhat crossed to make the golden image swim. But it vanished suddenly and with a triple click as Mr Carew cleared his throat, returned entirely to the present, and said, 'Well, Charles, I suppose you would like to rest after your journey? Yes, I am sure you would. And here is the paper, if you would like to look at it . . . through the door.'

When Charles opened the door he had a stupefying impression of blindness and of being unable to breathe, for instead of the air and light that had always met him on the other side of every door there was a curtain; and since his eyes were unprepared for anything so near they could not make it out. An arm stretched suddenly over his head and he automatically dodged under his upraised elbow, but it was only Mr Carew reaching for the curtain. 'It is a portière, against the draughts,' said the deep voice on high as they passed through the dust-smelling folds. 'We thrust it aside on entering.'

He found himself alone, holding *The Times*, in a new room. Carew would come back at four 'when he had been to the Institute' and then 'they would have a cup of tea together and talk over the future.' The heavy brown curtain had fallen at the word 'future' concealing cousin Carew; but almost at once it stirred and billowed; the enormous form partially emerged and looking upwards Charles met the queer, magnified pale glare full in the eye, all the time the huge voice was saying, with a factitious gaiety, 'Of course I need not say that I am sure nothing will be touched.'

So he stood for some time, quite still, while this unpleasant and even shocking introduction to the room receded into the past. It was a stark room, lit by the north light flooding in through a window whose panes were made of ground glass: this blind but shining quality in the window, together with the curtain that masked the door, gave the room and everything within it a very special feeling of insulation – a deaf and inner world. It was an improbable room, altogether outside his experience; and even the shining black horse-hair couch (the only familiar object) was inhumanly tall; but once it was accepted as a room he saw that it possessed extraordinary attractions. He walked over to the couch, on which it was supposed that he would recline, sipping *The Times* and dozing, until four o'clock; it was high and slippery, but at the second attempt he scaled it, and sat there dangling his legs. So much was required of him in politeness to the fiction that he was tired after his journey: he also unfolded *The Times*.

There were many objects he had never seen before. Cradled in its basket under the main laboratory bench stood a carboy of brimming vitriol, while above it nitric, hydrocyanic, oxalic, hydrochloric, malic, formic, hydrofluoric and even prussic acid offered their possibilities of fuming experiment and sudden death in a neat range of Winchester quarts. On a shelf to the right of the bench a jar of caustic soda provided the same end by a different means: the strychnine was on the top of the cupboard, however, and could be reached only by standing on a chair.

Then again, the incubator held cultures and living tissues, the fruit of months of preparation – a hand playing with the long rod of the thermostatic control, or even fondling its shining counterpoise, might falsify the results of a whole series of experiments; and apart from the incubator there were scores of appliances, instruments, switches, dials and complicated arrangements of glass, all functioning, all vulnerable.

He listened. One did not live with Mrs Clapp for long without becoming tolerably sly, and he listened for a good while. Yet this was little more than an automatic precaution: he did not really believe that cousin Carew would lurk in the passage, creep to the door, silently turn its oiled handle and fling it open to catch you in some forbidden pursuit, such as staring in the looking-glass. Cousin Carew would indulge in any excesses he chose (subject to the rules), seeing that he had the power to do so; but he was so much larger than even Mrs Clapp's most spiteful predictions, so bodily vast and spiritually overwhelming, that these excesses would be of the Sodom and Gomorrah kind or nothing at all – fire, brimstone and annihilation at the least; nothing trifling like waiting at the door.

Still, he listened; and it was not until ten minutes had gone that he slipped down and began his first, tentative, tip-toe exploration of the room. It was a five-sided space with the couch flanked by glass-fronted bookshelves along one wall, and as he proceeded anti-clockwise round it he came first to the long, high microscope table, with its tall and unlikely stools. There were two microscopes on it, one under a glass bell. Next came the curtain that hid the door, then a white cupboard with a white metal trolley in front, then a bare expanse of the third wall. Here was a picture, the only one in the room: a large picture in which an immense bearded figure waded knee-deep in the sea, bowed under the burden of a curious slab, which he was carrying from right to left. No one could say where he was carrying it to, but he was going very carefully, in order to keep it flat, because the top of the slab was a garden: you could consider the slab as a kind of stone tray, a gigantic tray, of course, since the garden was big enough to have trees growing in it, and it was filled with people of the ordinary size. They wore robes. Some were dancing, but the nearest were lying on their sides, letting water pour out of jars over the edge. They were holding on to the jars in a loose sort of way, but they were not really paying attention: they were not even looking where it was going. They did not look over the edge: nor did anybody else up there. Perhaps they did not know that they were being carried.

How did they get water up there, being detached? And it was so silly to show it always pouring out like that: it would not last any time. Some of it might be dribbling on to the giant. Was he meant to be cousin Carew? How would they ever be able to renew their water? Perhaps when he had waded a bit farther he would come to an enormous rock and smash them all down on it. If it was meant for cousin Carew, why the beard?

It was an unsatisfactory picture really, and presently he moved on, still undecided. Here was the beginning of the long white-tiled laboratory sink that swept round the shallow angle to the fourth wall of frosted glass, where the main bench showed its array of laboratory glass – retorts on tripods, upright tubes clasped in iron tongs, red rubber tubing, corks with glass tubes coming through them, bottles joined by the middle, by the neck, by the bottom. Bunsen burners. By comparison the fifth wall was dull: it only had the incubator, a microtome and a centrifuge that happened to have had its handle taken off.

His tour lasted some time, quite long enough for the peculiarly cut-off, contained atmosphere of the silent room to have impinged upon him and to have given him the beginning of the feeling of total privacy that was essential for glee.

The third time round he climbed the rungs of one of the stools and sat upon the horse-hair top – Mr Carew had a passion for black upholstery stuffed with horse-hair – looking at the microscope, the rows of test-tubes in their racks, each with its sloping field of jelly, speckled or striated, the rows of slides, the parade of dropping-bottles, aligned by size from the right and all pointing their noses to the left. Basic Fuchsin, he read on the nearest, while he was wondering how to look down the microscope without touching it. What was Fuchsin, and how could it be Basic? The microscope was not very difficult; he had but to kneel on the stool and put a hand on each side of the stand to have his head poised right over the eyepiece. But it was a disappointing tube. At first he could see nothing whatever, and even when after long peering he made out a dim grey round down there, with the shadow of his eyelashes crossing and recrossing its surface, it was not very exciting: and if it had not been for the potency of the words, 'Looking through a microscope' he would not have hung over the unlit instrument for two minutes, let alone a quarter of an hour.

The picture yielded no more at the second examination than it had at first. The water still poured in unaccountable vexing waste from the jars, the gigantic cousin Carew forged carefully on through the deep, bent under his careless load. Surely he would chuck the whole thing off when he got out really far? It was impossible to tell from his expression, however, which was inscrutable and old.

He was moving slowly away from the picture, bowed, with lumpish motions, looking inscrutable and old, when he noticed a small looking-glass by the sink. He hurried to it and leaning over the sink to bring his face as close as possible to the glass he gibbered silently for a while. Then he dragged down the lower covers of his eyes until a great deal of red showed, and afterwards he stretched his face sideways with the palms of his hands hard and long so that his eyes almost vanished and the tight skin over his nose and cheekbones showed yellow against the bluish tumescence of his distorted lips; this was his most accomplished face; but before it reached perfection and the utmost limit of the stretch his eyes always lost their ability to see and he could only guess the ultimate effect.

He throttled himself dull purple with his tie, investigated the gaps in his teeth, and settled down to his usual inter-course with this rare, most treasured and best companion – rare, because of Mrs Clapp's aversion for mirrors.

He leant close and imitated Mrs Clapp for his own applause. Tightening his lips and narrowing his eyes he said, 'Now then, now then . . .' But his invention failed him and for his portrait he fell back on a list of words that typified her: twee, dainty, all things bright and beautiful, people like *us* (with a leer of idiot complacency), doyley, the conven-ience, let us see if *Charlie* can Be the little gentleman, I wish to complain to the manager. Then he said his oaths aloud, even fung: 'Fung Mrs Clapp.' His reflection applauded this daring flight, but the words were hardly out before he felt uneasy; two of them were blasphemy and they had been clearly said, not mumbled with the possibility of excuse.

This momentarily chilled his enjoyment; he turned away from the looking-glass and that mirror-world in which he was somewhat compromised, and moved into the clear middle of the room, where he spun until he was dizzy – the best way he knew of changing an unwelcome flow of thoughts and averting the evil chance.

Staggering, he reached the main bench along the blind but luminous window, the bench with the retorts, the air-pump, the flasks, phials, alembics and tubes, and the Bunsen burners. One of these had a pilot-light, a minute plume of stiff blue flame, and laying his head sideways on the zinc-covered bench to steady himself he saw that the flame possessed a little ghost of dancing air, like the few candles he had been left alone with. They had been utterly absorbing: he had burnt the matches from the tray of the candlestick, burning them at each end and dipping them in the pool below the foot of the flame so that they would burn again, on and on, until at last the candle died, a tiny blue flame with no yellow left, a bishop's hat, floating on the pool right down in the socket – a flame that would become too small and delicate to be touched or helped with the charred end of a match, a flame that would go on nevertheless, existing with no more light than would just illuminate the pool of wax and the busy circulation in it, detached almost entirely from the wick, but which finally, for no reason – certainly for no incautious breath of his – would gather itself from below, draw up a hairsbreadth higher and vanish upwards, leaving him stiff, cold and still partially hypnotized.

The flame of the Bunsen burner was pretty good: it lacked the supernatural qualities of the candle, but in some ways that was just as well; and in active burning powers and robustness there was no comparison at all. He had defeated his conscience at once: his hard-learnt caution had resisted a little longer, but step by step it had given way, and now, waiting for the mercury in the thermometer to creep down, he placidly directed the tongue of flame against the zinc table-top. Again the metal sweated mysteriously under the heat: it should have dried, in the course of nature, but it sweated, and the drops, running viscidly into one another, smelt vile like a gas-works. To his right lay the unscattered ashes of what little he had found to burn in this aseptic place – two matchsticks, half an inch of discarded rubber tubing, a little paper, some horse-hair and the chips from a pencil sharpening – and to his left the thermometer, with its obedient life.

It was an unusually long thermometer, graduated to four hundred degrees, and by now he had perfected a ritual in which he made the quicksilver mount stage by stage to the very top, to the unmarked space above the highest score. He had done it a great many times already, driving it up by the power of the flame, with a continuous murmur of command and warning; and now he was waiting to do so again. Unfortunately, it would not come down nearly as quickly as it would go up, and that meant too long a wait between the necromancies.

It had just been lying there, this thermometer, naked on the bench, eighteen inches from the burner with the pilot-light; and even now it was not above a foot from its original position. Long before, when his caution was still jagging across his pleasure, he had made sure of his retreat: he had only to turn the tap with one motion, put down the thermometer with another and make three steps towards the couch to be as safe as if he had lain there all the afternoon.

It would be cool now, he thought, setting the burner down on its base: but it was not; the silver still showed quite high in the stalk, and its downward movement was now so slow that it could hardly be seen at all. He blew on it and the mercury shrank a little: it had nearly reached the thirty mark, and when it did it would only have ten more to go: the ritual could begin when it reached twenty, the point at which he had found it. But how it crawled.

With some surprise at his stupidity in not thinking of it before, but with more pleasure at having thought of it now, he darted over to the sink, dribbled the cold tap on to the thermometer and saw it contract to ten degrees.

He was so pleased. This would allow him to command the quicksilver in both directions, to say 'Zadkiel, sink down' as well as 'Zadkiel, rise.' He filled a beaker at the tap and carried it carefully to the bench, holding the thermometer across his mouth.

He turned the burner high, and hurrying his liturgy he made the mercury race up count by count: at the end, on the four hundred mark itself, he was quite mute. His sallow face was pink and his eyes shone as he held the tube, now a solid bar of mercury, over the cold water. His gaze was fixed on the silver column as he lowered the bulb into the beaker: as soon as it touched he would see the quicksilver shoot right down. Not breathing, he let it carefully to the surface of the water: there was a sharp hiss, the bulb and the lower inches of the thermometer shivered, and he saw the column separate into an unconnected row – dashes of mercury.

At first he could not understand what had happened. Then, in spite of the fragments of glass, he would not. It was too dreadful to be true; and he stood there motionless, quite ashy pale; his mind was so beset and so shocked, that for a long time he could not tell what he thought, nor what he felt except the presence of disaster. He stood there holding the tube very carefully, waiting for it to come right again: and more and more the awful suspicion that it might not ever come right flooded into him.

It still might not be true, or not wholly true: there was hope, he said when after the first full shock he was capable

of coherent thought; and softly he turned the Bunsen
burner out, tiptoed to the sink and with infinite attention he
poured the water off the quicksilver and the little mess of
glass.

He tried and tried again, but the pieces would not stick
with spit; the quicksilver would not run back into the tube
at all; and while he was pressing a piece of glass against the
broken end another two inches came away and shattered on
the floor. Yet still at the very bottom of his mind he believed
that something beautiful would happen that would enable
him to put the healed thermometer very gently down
exactly where he had found it and go and sit on the couch
until the end of the day. This belief vanished slowly, and he
did not see it flicker out; but immediately afterwards he
understood that the catastrophe was whole and real, and
that his attempt at piecing together the fragments could
never succeed.

He accepted this dully, and after one or two faint gestures
of protest he stopped even trying to complete the impossible
jigsaw: the pieces, ten large ones and innumerable fragments, lay arranged in front of him; what was left of the
quicksilver was in the beaker to his right, and the broken
thermometer lay behind the smallest fragments. All he had
to do now was to wait: in the exhaustion of his spirit he
felt quite numb, and now, if he had been a crying child,
he would have wept, with his head down on his arms. But
he was dogged still, and after a long time he began a sort of
little dreary joyless game of spillikins, arranging and re-
arranging the pile of fragments with the longest splinter.

A remote, muffled noise outside wrenched him into the
present with a tingling jet of fear, and he realized that he
was waiting for the end of the afternoon; that the end of the
afternoon was really coming; and that when it came the
door behind the curtain would open.

He hurried to the couch and sat on it, holding the newspaper, a symbol of obedience. If only, if only it had not

happened . . . There were moments when he could almost persuade himself that it had not or that it would all come right; but as the dumb wait drew on and on, nearer to the awful moment when the curtain would billow, heave and part, this insubstantial comfort died. In spite of endless denial he came to accept the disaster as a fact; with this acceptance the enormity grew even worse, and with a new sense of worry he feared that perhaps he had broken the microscope too.

He had not: he went to it, and it was not broken. But what did that matter? It was no comfort. The thermometer was broken and the microscope might as well have been broken too: it made no difference.

What if he picked up the microscope and smashed it and the Basic Fuchsin too and all the painted bottles? And then smashed the ground-glass windows and found a way out? He stared round and round, breathing deeply.

He was feeling sick. He was going to be sick. For a long while he hung over the sink with the tap running: he took a drink in his cupped hands. Now he was very cold and his desperate apprehension was swallowed up in the misery of being sick: yet the first sound revived it, and now that the twilight made the frigid windows more important in the room his jangling nerves invented sounds outside: doors opening, steps coming nearer. It must surely soon be four o'clock?

Yet time went on and on and on. Shut away in that darkening room, sealed from the rest of the world, he felt that it had gone wrong, that it had gone wrong and stopped, as a clock will stop.

For a good while there had been no sound, and he was beginning to dull the edge of full reality again when with an appalling explosion a telephone-bell shrieked out.

It seemed to be coming from over by the window, but he did nothing: he stood in the middle of the room, clasping and unclasping his hands while the noise shattered his spirit.

Behind him the curtain swelled and parted and let in a stream of golden light with the huge dark man in it.

'In the dark! Why . . .' He heard the words mingling with the dreadful bell, the fast thumping strides, a little crash of glass and the click of the telephone.

'Hallo? Yes, but just hold on a minute. I'm in the dark and something has fallen over. Charles, put on the light, will you? By the door. To the right.' Screwing up his eyes against the glare he saw cousin Carew leaning on the bench, still vaster in his overcoat. 'No, nothing at all,' he was saying. 'It was only that I knocked a thermometer off the bench and trod on it. And a beaker. Nothing of any importance. I was afraid it might have been the ureometer, my Gerard's ureometer. My coat might have caught the ureometer. No, the ureometer . . '

The Lemon

A MAN who lives alone grows strange: and I have been solitary now, how long? Some years at least.

It is the peace he has, the room to develop. Most people are bound to observances; the clock if they are employed, the routine of a life in all events; but a man alone can live to himself, lie three days abed, work through the night, sit motionless for hours, think in the way he likes. He grows unlike the others; for a man must think to grow, and thought is a slow process, a cumulative thing that grows: you must not check it. But meals, visitors, and hot and cold, set hours, do check it. They dissipate the cloud, the haze inside which your mind can turn. The solitary man grows strange; but it is the strangeness of an adult among children.

It must be the right kind of man, of course. It is not every man who can live by himself: two of the other painters here are mad. With old Dupont it is probably a question of senility, no more; but Laforge is mad directly. He goes by with a quick shuffle, just not breaking into a run, and there is such a look of concentrated unhappiness on his face that if it were not so annoying you would be desperately sorry for him – providing you thought there was still a 'him' alive behind that closed-in, wretched face. The people in the street turn after him and stare. They make the usual gesture, and although they have seen him for a long time now they watch him avidly to find him worse. Presently they will shut him up, no doubt.

In madness, I understand, there is nearly always this misery: not quite always, but certainly very often in the kind of solitary madness that I am thinking of. There is always – and this is the vital distinction – a loss of objectivity.

They also lose (a consequence, I think) whatever sense of humour they ever had. And that I do possess, as strong as it was when I was a child, to whom so very many things are funny, even the sound of words. The last time I had dinner with the Lemaîtres, Marie said that someone or other had a sponge factory, and the words themselves were so absurd – not the meaning, the words intrinsically – that they made me laugh and laugh and laugh, although I did not want to. I did not want to hurt Marie (I do not know her well, nor yet Lemaître) and it was not an explicable joke, *fabrique d'éponges*. It depended on the *i*, long and high, and the round *ponges*, and the particular air of solemnity. But I could not stop, though I turned my eyes away from their ludicrous wondering faces, faintly displeased behind their polite smiles: I swallowed a mouthful of scalding soup, dropped my napkin: but it was no good, the tears came into my eyes, and when the *fou rire* gained the others and they began to giggle too, I burst out and gasped and gasped until I was nearly sick and could not breathe. We said *fabrique d'éponges* and howled: sometimes we could say no more than *fab* . . . It wrecked the dinner: but my God I laughed.

However, that is only a minor point: the essential is the insight, objectivity. I have watched a clock for hours, the wonderful peace of the pendulum's swing, and I have seen it swing left and right, left and pause, back across the nadir, rise and pause. And stop. Stop poised up on the right until I have let it go, to swing and tick, swing and tock. But all the time I have known just what it was, that my mind was spinning free and time was not. No loss of insight there.

And I have looked at my naked feet, bony and long on a chair before me, and I have seen the stigmata form, and from each crimson wound a rose.

Yes, I know that road: I am quite clear there. That is not what can do you any harm, nor make you unhappy. On the contrary, I should say, all things summed up, that I was

a very happy man. I was less so when I still roved after
women, when that hunger and excitement drove me out;
when a dark warm evening came and I was restless, could
not settle until I had defined my need. But that was long
ago. I have had all the common girls here, and some others
too; Thérèse and Rose, Conchita and that Denise who made
me ill. The fair one – Marie-Claire? Denise again? I never
could recall her name. But since the fire went out, I have
been happy, in my way.

Yet so much hangs on what you mean by that. A calm
euphoria, an isolation: that is what I mean. A burrowing
in, deep, deep down until you reach a kind of peace glowing
inside a haze.

Sometimes it will not work; something goes astray. This
morning it was like that. I was reading, and between the
paragraphs the associations piled up, so that I was thinking
on two or three separate levels: that is normal enough;
every man does it who talks, and at the same time thinks of
what he is going to say next, and at the same time bears in
mind that he must not stay more than five minutes because
he has an appointment, and at the same time sees a creature
flying and says in some inner compartment, 'That is a wasp:
it might sting.' It is normal, and with practice it can be
developed.

As I say, I was following out these associations, and that
usually settles down to a line of wordless thought which goes
on while I read and after I have stopped, reaching, in the
end, my happiness far down.

But this morning, the associations grew and multiplied;
they were obstrusive, unmanageable, and I became confused. Generally they act as planes, planes that dissolve, one
behind the other, like my painting: though that is an
inaccuracy, because like the sheets of colour in my work,
they are not *behind* one another – that is not the relation at all.
They are *different* planes; but I will not dwell on this.

This time there were two other features, both quite

familiar, but now they were out of place. The first was that the whole thing was a game, a pretence that I could stop at any minute. The whole thing, my sitting there, my being in that room, my existence indeed; that was a game. This feeling I have known for years and years, and sometimes I think it first arose from some dishonesty, from some insincerity and forcing of emotion. When I was a very young fellow I played at being in love, saying the words, making the gestures, while my heart pumped blood hard through my veins and real tears blurred my vision; but all the time I had a faint (not always so faint) glimpse of myself from a viewpoint generally in a corner of the room and I would say something more or less satirical – my corner-self would say it internally. Later, a good deal later, when I finally abandoned figurative painting, I worried about the honesty of my work, and I believe the worry, the question at all, was a proof that somewhere I had cheated, worked myself into an attitude where the self standing in the corner could rightly smirk and say 'Oh behold the new-born Braque.'

There was more to it than that; much more, but these partial causes are very remote now. The important thing is that at times the feeling is very strong (it hardly ever leaves me entirely) and then my surroundings seem so impalpable, such a hollow pretence, that it makes me if not unhappy, at least confused. Ordinarily it is not unpleasant, rather the reverse: one can pretend to be going for a walk, to be talking in a friendly, sociable manner, to be living very cheerfully – it simplifies daily life very much. No: what I have said might have been the cause was not the cause at all. The two pretences are quite distinct, different in nature. The first was dishonesty; the second is not – it is a feeling that the illusion is slipping away.

The second thing that spoiled my reading and its consequences was a sense of having been there before. The words had a vexing half-familiarity, though it was a new book: now and then a whole phrase would be entirely known and (what was more troubling) my own reflection on the known phrase would come out pat like a sentence learned by heart. I knew what I was going to read, what I was going to say on discovering that I knew it, and my own rejoinder to that second discovery: and so on, seven deep.

My own comfortable, favourable mist or haze was now a fog. I no longer felt that at the worst I had only to stop pretending, stop playing this private game, to stop existing. I was getting lost, losing control: and to reassert the discipline of my mind I deliberately read a page of the book. That did very little. I got up and washed my hands and face.

I was sorry now that my cat had gone: I had had an affection for that distant creature although I knew it was a descent into emotion; and now I was sorry that the cat was not in the studio. I would have opened it a tin of fish if it had been there, and doing that would have been valuable.

I looked at the painting that I had up on the easel and I began to work on it mechanically. Soon I had spoiled the canvas, and I let my hand draw criss-cross lines.

The base and cause of the wretched state of my mind, I found, was a sort of dream that I had had in the night. It was about my neighbours.

They were good neighbours, below, in front and on each side. They were often very kind to me – took in parcels, told me the news of the quarter when we met, and when my cat was still here they were kind to her, too; gave her milk. I do not think they approved of my girls, but that was long ago, and I had always been very quiet, even then. They were working people, kind, sensible, tolerant. Good people, my neighbours: all except the man and woman who kept the restaurant on the ground floor. They were a bad couple; the man a flashy, smarmy-haired little pompous rat; the woman a short-legged, hard-faced shrew of about forty. I went there at first because I thought it would save trouble, and they gave me an omelette with a cockroach in it. They drank heavily, quarrelled and screamed until dawn sometimes. Their place was frequented by their friends and by foreigners on the spree, and they bawled and sang and shrieked above the blaring radio until four or five in the morning. The man was odiously ingratiating: the woman too: she had a high screaming laugh, more truly metallic than I have ever heard from a human throat. She could let it rip at will, and she did whenever anybody else laughed. It was quite false: she had never really laughed in her life except at a puppy drowning.

They had a waitress whom they did not pay: she made her living from tips and by whoring with the customers. All the sporting men of the place went there after her and you could hear them out-manning one another in deep voices and whooping cachinnation. She was a big wench, fairly pretty, crammed with high spirits. I would have had nothing against her at all, if she had not sung: but she did sing, every morning until lunchtime, while she cleaned the restaurant. She sang very loudly, very affectedly – she was being the quaint pretty girl scrubbing floors and not minding it, I believe – and on one note only. It was a false note, and the damned songs she sang penetrated windows, shutters, floors, everything.

There they were, a pretty crew; and the man had one trick that irritated me more than all the rest. He had an ugly little signboard hanging on the wall, pointing to his restaurant, and every time he passed it he would set it straight. The gesture, indicating ownership, importance, the right to touch, was so automatic that he would do it without even looking to see whether the sign were straight or not. Sometimes he would go out, touch it without looking, and come back. I could have borne anything but that.

To return to this kind of dream of which I have spoken. They were making more noise last night than usual. I wondered whether my neighbours in front would get angry enough to throw a bottle: they did sometimes when the din had been intolerable for many hours past midnight. I felt angry for them: they and all the people around were working families who got up early. Many and many a time have I seen them come out, cross and bleary, robbed of their sleep and robbed of their full day's power by the screaming hooligans below. As time went on I grew angrier on my own account.

Then I was thinking in my chair for a long while. In separated waves the noise pierced through, but when I got up to find my bomb I was no longer angry. I was far within myself, but I recalled my anger, for myself and for those other people, and I examined it: it was very red, emotional and raw: roughly triangular.

My bomb was one of the small kind that we used to call a *citron*. I do not know its technical description, but it was a hand grenade, shaped like a lemon. I had kept one, because I liked its form. I found it in my box of different shapes, kicked off my slippers and went quietly downstairs. As I went down the shrieks and laughter increased. In the lobby inside the front door (it is always open except in the winter) there are the fuse-boxes for the whole house. I drew the white porcelain bridge that controlled the restaurant's electricity, and as their lights went out I heard the huge, anticipated shriek and the waitress's unbridled scream as one of the men grabbed her in the dark.

The electricity is always breaking down in this street, and everyone has candles ready. I waited a moment until I saw the dim glow reflected, and then I went into the street. In the darkness outside the open restaurant door I stood and looked in: the girl was out of the room; the rest were gabbling about a second candle. They were all drunk. The woman let out a burst of her cackle and I drew the pin. It was, I remembered, a seven-second fuse, so I counted five before lobbing it in. It was remarkable that the people looked at the bomb as it landed, and not towards the place it came from, as I had expected.

It went off with a great orange flower of light that

blossomed momentarily in the whole street. I pushed back the electric fuse and went silently upstairs, pursued by the familiar smell of dust.

There was no possibility of detection. All the neighbours would be at their windows, not looking down the stairs.

Now the thing that worries me about all this was the moral aspect. The withdrawal of the fuse was an act of lunatic cunning that would never have occurred to me as myself. I do not think that I even knew which was the right box. But the fact that I did withdraw it is terribly significant: at some time in my journey downstairs my play, my pretence of being a man – and hence my control – must have merged into a sense of reality and uncontrol.

This train of thought must have started in the morning before I sat down with my book, it must have started unconsciously when I looked down into the street and saw a mess of plate glass still heaped in the gutter and the people staring: and it must have been that that wrecked my reading, a deep, well-founded distrust of that single element in the dream – dream or physical reality, it does not matter which.

The essence of the matter is that the action of withdrawing the fuse was the action of a psychopath. And the consequences are bad. I do not mean the bodily consequences: detection is impossible. No; the consequences of an action that one recognizes as undoubtedly psychotic are that one must take measures against the possibility of a repetition: if once the lapse is established, to go on living would be criminal in an honest man.

And it is so soon established: one question is enough. 'Did you draw that porcelain bridge that holds the wire, and did you leave it so that you could push it back in the dark?' If the answer is yes, you must then say 'You did not know where the fuse box was: you know almost nothing about electricity. But your unconscious mind had noted the place and the function of the bridge; long ago, perhaps. It formed an intention, against the time when it could take over control. The intent was criminal. The thing that formed it must be cut off. The only moral issue now before you is the recognition of this fact.'

The Last Pool

'This is the last pool,' he said again, as he stood by the side of it with the water running over the toes of his waders. He had said the same thing at each of the five pools below it, and he had meant that if he did not catch a trout he would go home. Each pool in turn had yielded nothing, not even a rise to save the face of his resolution. Each time he meant it more, and now he meant it entirely: beyond this pool was a long flat stretch of river, difficult to fish and notoriously barren; to circumvent both it and the small private lake beyond meant a tedious hot walk in waders already too warm for comfort.

The last pool was certainly the best pool for size and looks; it stood high above a series of chaotic rapids, and an almost unbroken rim of rock enclosed it. At the top end the river came clear over a wall of black basalt four or five feet high, curving over in green water before it broke into two main cascades that came down in foam to the pool. Even now, after weeks of drought, the top quarter of the pool was white, and the water had a menacing roar to it. The outlet was one single column of racing water, a broad mortal jet that came through a black gate of rock in the pool's lower rim; it was from this that it had its name of Goileadair, or, as some said, the Kettle. The sides of Goileadair were sheer-to, and down the middle of it was a shingle bed, piled there by the two competing falls above. The highest part of the shingle was out of the water now, and quite dry.

There was a sombre air about this last pool – little colour, for the valley just here narrowed to a gorge with a great deal of naked rock to its sides. The Scots pines that had taken footing in the crag to the left showed darkly above, and the flash of the falling water accentuated the black polish of the half-sunken rocks. In Conan's time they drowned lepers here.

The gorge was beautiful, this man, this James Aislabie, observed to himself; but it was a harsh, grim kind of beauty, God forbid. He sat down on one of the smooth rocks that marked the end of the pool, the edge of the cleft that let the water out; the river slid fast and silently between these rounded edges, its surface curved and tense. It ran over his dangling feet with an insistent pressure and a grateful coolness; and in ten minutes the all-pervading roar that filled the gorge no longer reached the threshold of his hearing.

At the top end a yellow wagtail perched on a flat stone and stood bowing there and bobbing, and as James Aislabie watched the bird – a fine bird in the glory of his feathers – a fish leapt out of the foam a little to the one side of it. It was a small white fish, a sea-trout of perhaps half a pound or less, but it was a sight pleasant enough to a man who had fished long hours in the heat of the day without the sight of a fish at all.

All day long the weary length of the river, with its difficult, reed-grown banks lower down, and the beat of the sun on his back: the disastrous lowness of the water, with its shining surface and his cast lying awkwardly curled upon it, and his hot boots and the grinding strap on his shoulder. The bad, short, laboured casts as his arms grew more and more tired, the glare on the water as his eye followed the place where his fly ought to be, and the swirling water. When he lay in bed thinking about fishing he did not recall these things, nor the flies cracked off, pulled off, dropped, lost high up in trees.

He considered the best way to fish this pool, and he thought about changing his fly. He had no confidence in the fly he was using and none in the only other fly he had left, which was far too big. However, he cut off the one and tied on the other: it was more a gesture of piety than anything else. The name of the fly escaped him; somebody's Fancy, or possibly Indispensable, he thought, as he pulled the knot tight round the black, shining eye. It seemed but decent to do the thing correctly, although his belief in his motions had almost wholly gone.

His faith in the day's fishing had gone in three stages. At first, on the flat, easy stretches of the lower river, he had been keenly expectant, had made each cast with extreme care: he knew that some fair sea-trout, two- and three-pounders, had been caught within the week, and he hoped with each new cast that he should see the white flash of a turning fish and hear the scream of his reel. Then as the hours passed he had begun to hope rather desperately for just one fish, one, to save him from the wretchedness of having nothing at all. He pictured to himself the beauty of the fish, its gleaming sides, its black spots, the square tail and the fine, strong head, the heft of a good one dead in his hand. The vision grew clearer and more desirable still as he became more and more certain that he was going to catch nothing. It seemed, towards the end of the day, so very unlikely that any fish should want to take an artificial fly tied to a piece of gut; it was so improbable that there were any fish in that river, that if it had not been for some nagging persistence in the back of his mind he would have gone home about tea-time.

The feathers were smoothed, the cast was tried; he stood up and worked out a good line, facing the falls at the top of the Goileadair. His arm was rested, and he cast well; the line shot handsomely through his fingers, and the new fly dropped into the eddy at the outer side of the right-hand fall. It settled for a moment while the current carried down the slack; Aislabie's hand, as though it had an eye, took the line and drew it in, while he stared after the racing spot on the surface that should cover his fly. He was just about to lift his line off the water when some tiny variation stopped him. Was the cast moving a trifle across the current? It was, and the movement increased. With a quiet, smooth firmness it glided across and then upstream: there was a swirl under it that checked his quick strike. Aislabie stood there with the coiled line in his fingers.

'Wait. Oh wait,' he whispered, and he let a coil slip out through the rings.

Then came the pull; a firm pull, rather than the jerk of a little fish. Aislabie struck, with a straight, tight line; he struck too hard from over-anxiety. He had not finished the lashing upward stroke before his rod sprang to violent life. The rod top whipped down to the water, the two coils of line shot from his detaining fingers, and the reel gave a flying screech. In the middle of the pool a huge fish flashed three-quarters of its length into the air: it shook its head, poised there for an instant and fell sideways. In that instant Aislabie had seen every spot on it – the impression burnt itself in as a flash of lightning does. A silver, fresh-run cock-salmon, the heaviest he had ever seen alive. He had even seen the gleam of his cast between the strong beaked jaws.

Before the splash had settled it leapt again, clear of the water this time, and stood on its tail, worrying its head from side to side. Aislabie dropped his rod top: his hands were trembling so much that he could hardly find the knob of the reel, and his heart hammered in the back of his throat. His mind was devoid of coherent, conscious ideas: there was only a sort of cold exultation.

Then came a period of short, frenzied rushes across and across the pool, while Aislabie did nothing but endeavour to keep a tight line. This was not too difficult, as the fish went to and fro across the middle water, keeping roughly the same distance from him. His sense returned, and with it the depressing certainty that he was going to lose his cast for sure and probably most of his line as well. His reason conscientiously told him that only a silly man would hope to land a thirty-pound salmon with a short trout rod and fifty yards of line, a 3X cast and a little fly that a salmon should never have touched.

A salmon had no right to be there: only three, and small fish they were, had been taken in the river in the past twenty years. The top of his desire had been a two- or three-pound sea-trout, weighed by a friendly scale.

His body and the rest of his mind fought the salmon with every particle of skill and resource he had. A wild hope began to glow there in his heart; he put a stronger check on the fish, and the salmon responded with a strength that made the running line bite into his fingers.

So far the salmon had made no attempt to run up or down stream, and at present the only danger lay in the long, dividing finger of the bank of shingle between the incoming falls: if the run took the cast across one of its stones and then the fish were to turn, the cast would surely break. He became aware of this at the same moment that he saw the salmon turn just below the surface at the right-hand side of the pool and rush directly at the spit of shingle. Its shoulders were barely covered and he could see the wake it made, curving away right-handed to cross the tip of the spit. Plainly the salmon meant to go up into the deep hole at the foot of the left-hand fall. This would do two things: first, the curving rush would carry the line, if not the cast, over the bare rocks; and secondly, it would in all probability run the line clean off his reel, in which case it would tauten, stretch to the breaking-point in an infinitesimal fragment of time, break at the weakest point – he had a fleeting vision of the knot joining cast and line – and leave him with a still, lifeless rod.

As the wake neared the point, he leaned his rod out to the left horizontally and checked the racing line with all the force it could bear. The rod bent and quivered to the butt and the salmon's curve flattened perceptibly; it cleared the point several feet below the bare stones, but still the fish bore up right-handed. Aislabie could check no more. Suddenly he let go altogether, and his reel ran out free and screaming. He felt the knot between line and backing pass up through the rings, knocking as it went, and a bitter wave of disappointment welled up around his heart. There was very little backing – he had been careless – and that little was frayed and stiff. He could not gain any distance by wading into the pool; it was neck-deep a foot from where he stood.

The salmon took no notice of the slackened pressure; it sped on into the boil of the fall, to the topmost limit of the pool, and dived into the deep, slack water on the further side of the fall, the inward side under the falling water. There it lay, with its side and belly fins spread and its gills working violently: from time to time it worried, nuzzled against the water-worn rock, trying to dislodge the fly; but the hook was well home.

Aislabie stood there with a couple of yards of backing still on his reel, and for the first time he felt a reasonable hope. He had little enough ground for it, since the line was angled about a rock, and the salmon, should it wish to stay where it was, could not be moved. Still, ambition swelled up and took entire possession of him, so that he could hardly breathe. He saw the fish dead on the shore and wiped the loose scales from his hand – he would have to tail the salmon, for he had neither gaff nor net: he settled in his mind how to attach it to his bicycle.

The salmon, angered and disturbed by the thrumming that the taut line made in the fall, moved across the current and then quite slowly down into the quieter water. Aislabie left it alone until it was farther down than the shingle bed and then he bore gently on the line. The salmon, fiery as ever, hurled itself into the air twice, skittering along on its tail, and rushed straight across to the right-hand pool and back. It paused a moment, and then started a savage, exhausting series of short runs up and down the left-hand

half of the pool. Had it not kept to the far side, right under
the steep bank, the line would have crossed the middle bar
every time, and it would certainly have parted. As it was,
Aislabie, standing as high as ever he could, was just able
to keep a straight line and a continual slight check on the
salmon. Then, when the fish came over again to the hither
side, he could bear more strongly against the pull, and now
he felt that the salmon's first splendid flush of strength had
gone.

His greatest fear was that if he should manage to tire the
fish to a dangerous point, it would go downstream, through
the pouring lip of the pool, down the strong column of
water, and there, among the precipitous black rocks, he
could not hope to hold it for a moment.

Time rushed by, marked only by the passage of crises;
twice he had slipped on a mossy piece of stone, once the
salmon had bored into the only small patch of weed in the
pool, and many times his line had dragged perilously over
the bare rocks. Long ago he had noticed, with a hurried
glance at his top ring, that the sun had left the trees. By
now he felt that he knew the fish intimately well, could
foretell its reactions, could think in front of it. It was a
stupid, angry fish, he thought, with little of the sharp wit
of a trout: a clever fish would have been off in less than five
minutes. His own reactions, the working of the rod, the
instant reeling-in, the varied check, were quite automatic
by now; he did not think of them at all. As the fish began to
tire in good earnest, to make shorter rushes, he pressed it
harder and harder, allowing no moment of rest. Often as it
turned he saw the white of its belly.

'It will go down any minute now,' he said, and with half
an eye he marked three loose stones. He shuffled one
between his feet, and when the salmon turned heavily down
the current he had it there to throw with his free hand. It
was his one chance, a remote chance, but his luck was with
him. The salmon was near the surface, just above the very

strong rush of current, and the stone splashed six inches from its nose. It turned and ran upstream.

Quite soon after this the salmon began to tire so much that it was rolling in the water, and he could draw it towards him ten and twenty yards before it would run. At last he brought it into the side, curved with exhaustion and seemingly half-dead. He towed it gently up the bank to the one place where the rock ran down to within a couple of feet of the surface. With slow, blundering haste he changed his rod to the other hand, knelt down, muttering 'Calmly, calmly . . .' and made a foolish, impetuous grasp at the salmon. His fingers slipped incapably on the scales, and the salmon shot away with enormous power. The rest and the touch of his hand had renewed its courage and strength. He had known it, he said, and a lowering premonition of failure had been upon him as he knelt.

It was a weary battle now; his strength seemed to have gone into the fish. The consciousness of his own ineptitude tired him more than anything else. He realized now that his arms were as heavy as they could well be, that his reeling hand was about to be seized with a cramp, that he was going to make some last fatal error.

With a headstrong wilfulness, he bore on the salmon, disregarding his frail, frayed cast. The fish sank in the depths, and he pumped it out with the force he would have used with tackle fit for a salmon. His foolishness answered; the salmon made a last flagging run, tried three leaps, each weaker than the last, and lay drifting on the surface.

Now that he could see victory, Aislabie's desperate courage left him; he wasted vital time gaping, tied in an agony of indecision. His body and mind were so tired that he could hardly think.

The salmon came drifting down on the current on the near side of the pool. It was not going fast, for it was not in the main stream, but to one side of it. The fish passed him, and he stood impotently staring: it was downstream of him now, drifting towards the out-pouring fall, drifting faster. A queer eddy took the inert body, swirled it out of the current into the slack water of an overhung bay just to the one side of the fall's top.

With an awakening gasp he came out of his trance and ran heavily down the bank to the rock over the bay. He dared not draw the salmon along the bank now, so near the strong current, for he had left it so long that its strength might well be reviving, and one stroke of its tail would carry it into the run, over the edge and away. He knew that he must tail the fish there as it lay or lose it.

The rock on which he stood overhung the water by four or five feet; three feet down, below the usual high-water mark, a narrow sloping ledge jutted out. The fish was on the top of the water, filling this little cut-off basin, a demi-lune made by a backward swirl from the fierce stream that ran at right-angles to its mouth. He put his left foot down to the water-polished ledge – there was not an honest sharp edge of rock anywhere – put his right leg out behind and knelt on the smooth rock, facing up the pool. His right hand, holding his rod, stretched as far as it could over the flat top on which he had been standing.

He was oppressed by a sense of strong, present danger, and when he was in position he paused to collect himself. Peering down, he saw the fish from its dorsal fin to its tail; its head was under the rock and out of sight. It had sunk lower, and now lay in some two feet of water. Just above the tail fin he saw a faint band of lighter scales, the place where his hand had grasped before.

Now he let his left arm down to the water, and as he touched the surface he felt his left knee move. There was a patch of dark wet moss under it, and the rubber of his waders was slipping gently on it, downwards. The movement was very gradual, but the slightest motion of his body increased it. He brought his hand back to steady himself, but all his weight was on his left knee, and his hand found no resting place to thrust upon. He put his rod down, quite gently, for any abrupt movement would be fatal, and sought with terrible eagerness for a hand-hold; there was none anywhere in the compass of his reach. His right elbow stayed him for a moment, and by a huge muscular contraction he seemed almost to recover his poise. But his elbow could not grip on the mossy rock; the tuft of moss and grass on which it relied slid from under it, and he felt his weight swaying over on to his unsupported left side. He knew he was falling then. It was quite impossible to get his balance again, and even the smallest movement made him slide a minute, sickening, irrecoverable distance. His right hand, as though working by itself, still searched every inch of the smooth rock for a hold. There was none. He slid further. His whole body was tense to the extremity of its power, and the tension was unbearable. It was a relief when he fell at last – he no longer had to do anything now; it was decided for him now. He observed that his reason was working perfectly well although he was terrified and sweating with the fear of death.

'Right,' he said aloud, and let himself go. His hand, already under water and within a foot of the salmon's tail, dropped right on to the lighter patch of scales: he gripped with a kind of furious reaction just as his face hit the water and his mouth and nose filled chokingly.

The salmon gave a vast, galvanic lunge which momentarily checked his downward fall so that his body was asprawl when it hit the dark racing water. His face was set in a horrible grimace, but his fragmentary thought 'Oh God, the speed . . .' had no horror in it.

It was like coming out of an anaesthetic. He was quite happy, and he was aware that he was conscious before he opened his eyes. As he had supposed, there were people around him, and they were talking, although at a great distance still. He looked placidly at the grey shingle alongside his cheek and somewhat out of focus because of its nearness, he saw the battered head of the salmon.

They were wrangling softly about where the priest was to be found, and Dr Niel said again, 'I tell you he will certainly be at Tobin's – we sent for him – my own patient, for all love. Hurry now, Jack, will you? You can take the poor man's bicycle from by the bridge . . . Surely to God it must be the biggest fish that ever ran up this river.'

Aislabie smiled secretly: a voice said, 'He has come to,' and another, so anxious and kind, 'Can we ease you, Mister, as you lie?' The doctor was speaking too in a professional voice; but Aislabie could not bring himself away from his deep innermost glow; he smiled again, and drew in the smell of the fresh-run fish.

The Curranwood Badgers

MR BURKE had a pack of foxhounds and he drank a bottle of wine a day, but for all his glory he was never able to bully or flatter Joseph Quinn into growing citrus fruit in the William and Mary orangery at Curranmore; so when the obstinate old Fenian died he imported a Welsh gardener, named by his aunt. She lived conveniently near to Holyhead, and she recommended Moses-Henry Williams from a personal knowledge of twenty years, during which he had made the thin acid ungrateful earth of Plas Pwll flower like Eden before the Fall, if as may reasonably be supposed Eden was planted with heathers of every variety, azaleas and rhododendrons.

In those days of depression it was hard for a man to find a place: the big houses were closing everywhere, Plas Pwll among them, and butlers, footmen, grooms, gardeners and valets joined the desolate queues outside employment exchanges; so Moses-Henry tore up his roots, left the gardens to go back to bramble, nettles and furze, with the yew-hedges spiring, bracken heaving up through the gravel and his frames vanishing in a sea of fool's parsley, and boarded the midnight packet with his son Gethin, their possessions done up with horticultural twine: a widower, alas, and he had never learnt how to pack, far less to wash, cook or sew.

A tearing-up of roots indeed. He had never travelled farther than Bala; he had never been out of the sound of his own language: he was a deacon in the chapel at Rhobell-y-Big (Strict Ebenezer), and he had relatives in all the hill-farms behind. It would have broken his heart, but for the rich Munster earth, the unlimited stable-manure, the warm soft air, his half-acre of glass, and the spontaneous ease with which everything grew, including the pineapple, the peach and the coveted orange.

For young Gethin it was harder still. He left his first and only love at Rhobell, his flame undeclared, without their having exchanged more than conscious looks and a fairing; and although he was kept hard at weeding his heart flew back across the sea to his native slates and the cold drifting rain, to the gaunt farmhouse that sheltered Angharad, and to the hay-barn where they had sat side by side, their hands almost touching, talking politely through the hours of an infinitely welcome storm from the west.

Then again, Gethin's schooling had been all in Welsh: his mind was monoglot, and the Irish household abashed him with their unhesitating flow of English, as pure as a book. Their ways, their food and the flatness of their country amazed him; and when he saw the men hurry out on Sunday to start a hare he felt the world's foundations crumble.

The cook, who had eighteen nieces to marry and all the young men emigrating in droves leaving nothing but wicked old bachelors behind, and who loved to see young people happy, took him to a ceilidhe. She had known a convert make an excellent husband, or a husband at least; and there was no time to be lost, poor decent young fellow. But Gethin could make nothing of the thumping music, the pipes and the fiddle, still less of the dances, the floor trembling under him; and although the girls were so fresh, sweetly-spoken and modest, he had nothing whatsoever to say.

His solace, apart from a knee-harp of his own manufacture, was the company of Mr FitzGibbon, the huntsman, himself a recent arrival in the Curranmore demesne, Aloysius FitzGibbon from Cork. He had travelled far out of Ireland, as a trooper in his youth, when there were horses in the cavalry regiments, and then as a hunt-servant to various

English packs: he understood much of what Gethin had to say, and as to the Welshman's Protestantism, he delivered his opinions at length in the kitchen. Between his wheezes, chuckles and parentheses on oecumenical progress ('the back of my hand to the priest the wrong way about, arsy-versy – give me fish on Friday and the comfortable Latin') the words 'an oppressed people too, so they are' and 'kept their language itself, so they have, by damn' recurred again and again; and it was understood that the constancy of the Welsh in one respect might to some degree compensate for their changeability in another, and that they were not so utterly damned as Orangemen or Freemasons. 'Though to be sure we must pray for them buggers now,' he said with a sigh, before coming back to the Welsh, 'great fellows too, in the poetry line'.

FitzGibbon was long past mark of mouth, and what with whiskey and bawling at hounds his voice was a creaking whisper: a short, broad-shouldered, round man with a scarlet face set in wrinkles of mirth. His riding was now largely a matter of balance, a continuous miracle, but he hunted Mr Burke's hounds with passionate zeal, with skill and success; he killed a wonderful number of foxes a year, and the death of each was a fresh joy to him, a triumph never staled. He loved almost everybody around him, a most affectionate creature, so much so that the Kingdom of Thomond was filled with his likenesses, some tall and others short, but none under ten, for virtue had been thrust upon him at last.

It was strange that he and Gethin should have taken such a liking, for Gethin had never seen a hound in his life, far less climbed on to a horse, and his soul shuddered at the scream of a hare. However, he loved Mr FitzGibbon, and often after a long day he would go to the kennels to help feed the hounds, facing the ghastliness of flayed cows long dead, hanging blue and rain-soaked in chains from a tree, the swollen sheep, the quarters of an ass.

His father disliked the dogs – Calvinism and foxhunting do not run together – but he could not dislike FitzGibbon when he came to their cottage in the evening and laughed and wheezed in the corner seat, a party of pleasure in himself; and when Gethin asked for a holiday to go and draw the badgers of Curranwood with the huntsman he did not object.

The badgers had been increasing these last few years: they were turning up in places where they had never been heard of, and many a fox had gone to earth in an unsuspected sett, or had retreated into the fastness of an old holt newly enlarged. The worst badgers of all, said Mr FitzGibbon, were those who lived in Curranwood; they were unreasonably prolific; they were dead-bent upon peopling the country with more of their kind – little doubt they were Jews. And if the poacher Edmund Colman were to be believed, they were rogue-badgers as well, taking pheasants' eggs, chicks, leverets, partridges, rabbits, poultry, even small lambs, for the love of God. Edmund was probably right, since he watched his rivals more attentively than the keeper could do, he being so taken up with trying to circumvent the whole Colman family and the Quinns and indeed most of the male part of the village.

It was a long stretch to Curranwood, over the Sliveen bog and into the hilly country beyond, and as the kennel-boy cried off at the last minute – his Da was not feeling quite well in his bowels, the typhoid maybe – it was not that he himself was afraid: he did not care for Curranwood at all; had often been to it free and volunteerly for eggs, when at school – Gethin walked there by himself. He was glad of the solitary walk, partly because it would lead him through a patch of sweet-gale on the bog, a reminder of home, but even more because he had a poem turning about in his head.

His steps helped to beat out the metre, and in the open country he tried how it would sound.

Over the Irish sea the moon hangs like a red hawk.
It has caught my heart as the red hawk catches
  a warm quivering mouse:
The small blood rains down.

The moon hangs over the Irish sea like a looking-
  glass.
Angharad, my eyes strain up till the tears rain
  from them:
When will they see yours shining there?

He varied it this way and that, inverting the lines,
shifting the pause; and it was not from want of labour that
the poem was still far from what he knew it might be – what
it had been indeed when he first dreamt it – by the time he
came to the place where he was to wait for Mr FitzGibbon.
But his mind was not in its best dispositions, being in a
forward-looking state of excitement, reaching out for the
events of the day. He had heard of badgers for ever, but he
had never seen one and he would have walked ten times
the distance for the off-chance of a glimpse. He was not at
all sure what drawing implied: he imagined it meant something in the nature of driving them away; but the abstract
notion of death caused him no particular concern.

The place where he waited had been called Curranwood
only these last few generations; before that it had an Irish
name, and people still sometimes called it by the rough
equivalent, the *kind* or *gentle* place, which was in itself a way
of avoiding the still earlier heathen name, one that referred
more particularly to the mound in the middle.

An ancient wood, one of the few remaining pieces of the
forest that had once spread so far over the island: it had
never been cut, never tended in any way in the past; and
it was left untended, almost unvisited now. It had not
changed since the last wolf in Munster retired there to die:
the returning Firbolg would have found it the same.
Occasionally Conn Leary, the quickset man, would grub

round the edge when he was pressed for an order, and the keeper looked through it at times; otherwise the wood was never disturbed except when Mr Burke's hounds came there, the earth-stopper, or guests desperately keen for a cock.

It was a mixed wood, seen from outside, with ashes in the place where Gethin stood, alders down by the stream, and hazel; but its heart was all oak and had been for ever: low spreading trees, from hollow shells a thousand years old to saplings or the springing twig of the year. Young trees and old: yet the feeling was one of immense and hoary moss-grown age. That was the first feeling. The next, following without a pause, was that the wood was curiously silent; and not only silent but hostile.

Gethin stood in an open place where a ghost of a path led in among the ash-trees, and when he had felt this uneasiness upon him for some time he put it down to the ashes, with their poisonous drip. Nothing wholesome would grow under ash-trees, he knew: he would move farther into the wood.

Beyond a slope studded with toadstools – violent trans-lucent slime-covered witch's jelly and a colony of white-boys, now in viscid decay – he came to a place where the trees stood wide enough for fern to grow; and as he sat there he wished he had not set out so soon. There would be a long wait now, and already his poem seemed flat and cold, not worth turning in his mind, far less saying aloud in this silence. He made another about foxes in a rigorous old metre, more an eisteddfod exercise than a poem; but even as an exercise it was not much good, and it had the word *silence* in it, which he disliked.

Presently he found that he was thinking not about how to avoid the word silence but about trees and how very much more alive they were than they seemed. No one was afraid of a single tree, standing by itself. Nor of a dozen: nor of an orchard: nor of any number of planted trees. But a grove, an old grove of say a hundred, might have its particular feeling, its own air inside it; and this was far more than a grove – a wood, and a very ancient wood.

All at once it occurred to him that what he was looking at, the trunks, the boughs, the twigs branching for ever, was not the true living part, the knowing and living part: they were only the creature's inverted lungs hanging there. The head, the being itself, was underground. A tree was certainly an underground creature, a thing of the dark; and its true members were the roots, intricate past imagination and creeping extremely fine far beyond the spread of the boughs.

And yet that was not right, either: a single tree was hardly a creature at all, not a being in itself: that was why it was not formidable. The whole wood, all these trees together with their roots mingling in the closest communion so that the entire floor was a network, *that* was the real being, huge, silent, a single, listening being.

No doubt it was worse when they were all of the same kind: the same message passing through. And here there was nothing whatsoever but oak. As he said *worse* he realized that he dared not move. His neck was stiff: it would be extremely dangerous to turn his head. His senses were all on the stretch and he could hear very slight noises, so slight that they accentuated the dark, living silence – a crack behind him and to the left, a rustling. But it was not the noises that frightened him: what it was he could hardly yet name, although the name flickered on the edge of his unwilling mind.

A pigeon came gliding in, landed above him; then catching sight of Gethin's candle-white face it clattered out of the tree with an explosion that nearly made him sick. Yet this broke the spell of rigid listening; and not long afterwards he heard a familiar sound in the distance, Mr FitzGibbon cursing Yellow William, the ass. At once his terror receded, dwindling back into the wood before him; he stood up

without the least precaution, and although one leg had gone
numb he hopped and stumbled along so fast that he was
there on the path as the ass entered the wood.

FitzGibbon had three couple of terriers with him and a
puppy he had brought back from its walker: a crowd of
everyday creatures, smelly and welcoming; particularly
Gethin's favourite dog, the little square bitch that shared his
supper and often brought her fleas into his bed, Biddy by
name. 'There you are, boy, God love you,' he said. 'Let's sit
down in the shade.' He wiped his scarlet face with his handkerchief, looked round and asked 'Where's Tom?'

'He is looking after his Da, who has the typhoid to his
bowels maybe.'

'He is looking after Bridey Colman more likely, the
jackeen. I'll cut him, by and by – put an end to his capers –
Jesus, Mary and Joseph, I can hardly spit for the heat.' He
sat down to wheeze under the ash-trees, and winked at the
ass's pannier, saying something barely coherent about
bottled porter, the fewer the better fare, a bite of cheese,
and mind the old crow now Gethin avick. When he had
gasped and drunk and grown cooler he said, 'Tell me a
poem, boy, till I drink up my porter.'

Gethin put Biddy off his knee, cleared his throat for the
right bardic moo, and said

> 'Little foxes at the bottom of the cliff,
> Young foxes playing in and out.
> I let my breath go at last
> And instantly they are old hard foxes, motionless.
> I breathe in again – no foxes there at all
> Only silence, and a feather turning in the breeze.'

The old man chuckled and said it was as good as the
Latin almost: would Gethin tip him the English of it, now?

As they passed up through the wood Mr FitzGibbon showed
Gethin the signs of the badgers, their high-roads, their

filth-pits, the places where they stood up like cats, sharpening their claws; he pointed these things out in grunts and wheezes, shouldering his way along the badger-path, and it was not until they reached the first sett that he turned round, took the iron bar and the spade and said pleasantly, 'I hope we kill the little old bugger in here. Young Crambo needs blood.'

This was the first time that Gethin had known for sure that death was of the party, though the zeal of the dogs might have told him so at the edge of the wood. He said nothing, but listened while FitzGibbon described the loss of a cub in this very place at the end of a day, a cub he had particularly wanted to kill because the young entry too needed blood, the tonic of the world. 'Cubs, now, you don't want to be massacring cubs or breaking their hearts – just split up the families – but some blood the young 'uns must have.'

It was a new holt on a hazel-bank, not at all obvious, because the freshly-dug earth hardly showed between the nut-trees; and then there were rocks too, which stopped the badgers mining far down. But FitzGibbon pointed out the tracks, the odd wisps of bedding; and in any case the terriers' passion showed that this was no ordinary place.

The chief entrance was between two rocks, and ferns covered the hole, sweet-scented ferns. FitzGibbon gave Gethin the dogs and went grunting down on all fours, parting the fern and thrusting his head in as far as it would go, as he sniffed for the reek of a fox. Now the terriers knew he was in earnest and they bawled louder still, scrabbling the earth, pulling like horses, strangling themselves. The huntsman raised his purple face and called out for Teague, and the minute the terrier was loosed (a low dog with a great lunt of a head, a primitive Sealyham) it ran to him silently. Aloysius picked it up, whispered privately into its ear, and put it to. Teague thrust straight in and vanished.

FitzGibbon listened for a while and then he called for

Biddy, the dog with the cruel scar on her face: she shot down after Teague and all at once the other dogs fell silent. They sat there at Gethin's feet, rigid, pricked up, trembling continuously, while the huge hound puppy wandered about, so deeply ignorant that it took no interest in anything but twigs and an odd bit of filth, like a child taken to Rome. Some underground noise set them shrieking again and one of the couples broke from his hold – he had no sort of authority over the dogs at this point, though they liked him. FitzGibbon caught them with an off-hand sweep and held them dangling as he listened below. Apart from a slate-pencilling the other two were quiet, and Gethin could hear Biddy's characteristic scream, muffled under the earth. Suddenly Teague reappeared, having come up from another hole. His hair was roughed the wrong way and his white had turned blackish-brown: he ran busily through the bushes.

FitzGibbon slipped another dog, Crambo. Time passed, poised between crisis and boredom, an attenuated war: sometimes there were thumps below ground, sometimes a dog showed unexpectedly before darting below. Then at last came Biddy's frantic marking voice and at once the noise redoubled as Teague joined her. FitzGibbon turned from the mouth of the holt and nodded in a pleased, significant manner, winking and jerking his head sideways. Gethin could not interpret the look at all, but he felt his excitement mounting.

The din came closer: the badger was beginning to drive the dogs, a heavy boar badger for sure, a hard fellow with a deadly gripe. Now FitzGibbon was calling down the hole – 'Loo, loo into him, boy. Break him and tear him, then. There's a Teague. Go to him, Biddy. Bind hard to him, boy. Both sides, both sides, d'ye hear me now?' – a continual stream of words, and oaths against the badger. But the badger drove them: Biddy came right out, with the red blood flowing, and Teague could not face him alone. He retreated; the noise died down. Now he was in a lower tunnel: he had thrown up a mound of earth, blocking the passage, and the dogs were the wrong side of it.

There followed a long, long pause, with nothing but muted scuffles and grunts below. In his excitement Gethin had edged right up to the huntsman and they exchanged nods at every renewal of the underground noise. Now they heard Biddy again, marking to him; she was keeping her distance, while the other dogs found their way through the maze. The badger was moving steadily along a tunnel that stretched away to the left: at first they could hear Biddy under their feet, then they followed the sound along and through the hazel-clumps to the outcropping rock at the back. Here she was joined by Teague and Crambo. Together they made a continuous din, and when they came to a stay, a stay proved by banging with the spade, FitzGibbon gauged the place carefully and clearing himself a space he drove down into the earth. His coat was off, his round back bowed to the work: the soil flew from the hole. His breath grew short, his face more scarlet still, the sweat ran fast, but his eyes were blazing and he never paused as he hacked through the roots and flung up the earth. A yard down his spade rang on a great flat stone: now the din was close and incessant, a growling and snarling beneath the higher-pitched roar. 'The crow,' said FitzGibbon, reaching behind him. He had the tip of the bar under the stone: he heaved it loose and then high on to its side. It swung up and Gethin saw his badger at last, the striped head lifted, eyes blinking in the sudden light.

Then they were all down on him. At the worst Gethin had not expected this – the harsh grunting of breath, the thudding, the blows; the silence under the terriers' din.

At last he looked again. Mr FitzGibbon was brushing the earth from his clothes, wiping his face on his handkerchief, his hands on the grass; the dogs were still round the badger, growling as they dragged its limp body this way and that over the ground. He turned his pleased, innocent, engaging old face to Gethin and said, 'If I hadn't fetched him a puck with the spade, he had Biddy destroyed, the way she was under him.' His voice was so much the voice of everyday life, so devoid of evil or wicked excitement, that Gethin felt the world come back into order, the hellish chaos fade like a nightmare. Surely all this was natural enough, part of the woodland scene? The big puppy was rolling on its back, biting the leaves on either side. But when Gethin tried to speak he found that his voice was not under control.

FitzGibbon picked up the spade and his coat and they left the trampled devastated sett. Speaking in snatches over his shoulder he said they would try the big holt, the place they called the Shee in the old days, a hundred years ago, before Saint Patrick or Nebuchadnezzar; not that he expected they should do much, it being as huge as the underground railway in London. 'Was you ever in London, boy? The wicked great city, with no kind acquaintance – not to be mentioned in the same day as Cork. Still it has this railway, runs under the ground.' But it would stir them up, the old thieves, and maybe persuade them to go on to Mr Costelloe's land: they hated disturbance. And indeed it was likely they might find an outlier and chop him before he got into the maze. 'Or labyrinth,' he added, after a pause.

Gethin, carrying the heavy crowbar, cold and hard, walked some paces behind; and as he walked the guilt pressed down on him like a physical weight. He had done a horrible thing: a great unjust wrong, and a hideous wrong. He was one with the Devil. And now he was walking along behind Mr FitzGibbon, going on to another such blasphemous sin. He had no power to call out that it was evil. And as his mind cleared so that he understood this, he also found his old dread growing upon him again, in spite of the company: the company that was no company – he was utterly foreign to them.

Mr FitzGibbon had stopped: they were at the main sett

and he was pointing out the features of it. 'That's the old Shee itself,' he said. A bald mound fringed with nettles and elder: a heap of grey moss-covered stones: all round, the ancient oak-wood, crowding in towards the central space, the trees standing so close they shut out the evening sky.

Innumerable generations of badgers had changed the symmetry of the great mound; innumerable generations had dug here, and the spoil-heaps themselves stood as high as a man. They were still digging too: in two or three places the fresh earth showed plain.

Gethin had no animosity towards Mr FitzGibbon, made no judgment on him or his dogs; he only felt a sick apprehension of what was to come. The day was turning in spite of him. There was nothing he could do and when FitzGibbon said should they go round to look at the queer old stone he followed without a word. FitzGibbon was telling him about his boyhood in Cork – not a local boy at all – *he* had not come off the bog – old-fashioned ways – and there they stood in front of a domed cylindrical stone, dark, a yard high, faintly covered with interlacing bands. As they reached it a magpie flew out of an elder and FitzGibbon broke off to stare for its mate. The minutes went by, and no second bird. 'By damn,' he cried, striking his spade into the ground. 'There's the end of our luck, the bloody old bird. The bloody, mongrelly bird.' Gethin heard him curse the wood, the rotting bloody old wood, and the dogs, the glum parcel of sods – no keenness, no fire in these dogs – they should be given a meal of mustard, once they were home. 'And you've lost your tongue, young fellow. Is it the colic so sudden, the gripes? But I dare say,' he added, good humour returning, 'I dare say you have a poem in mind.'

He paused, looking at the low yellow sky, and the silence gathered in: the dogs gazed up into their faces. Gethin's extreme distress had affected the bitch he liked best: the others had caught it from her – it was spreading fast. He had some vague notion of this, but how much of it was himself and how much the wood Gethin neither knew nor cared. 'I was going to tell you about that stone,' FitzGibbon said, 'but sure I'll do that another time.' And raising his voice to its habitual pitch he cried 'Hoick, a Teague, hoick a Biddy, get along forard. Hiyo, hiyo, hiyo. We'll try the first sett.'

It was a big open hole, unconcealed, the earth sandy and clean. He put Hector and Cutty to it, but they would own nothing there: went in, came out again with a busy, attentive look. He put them in again. This time they went a little farther before they came out, and while they were down Teague started to dig at a small hole to one side; he disappeared, and all at once Biddy let out an eager screaming, shriller than her usual note. Yet when she was slipped she made nothing of it at all: in and out all the time, whimpering – she seemed to have forgotten her trade.

'She had a kiss she didn't like the last time,' said Fitz-Gibbon without conviction. 'She prefers that kind by the post.' He peered and smelt at the little hole. 'It's the queer smell here, so it is,' he said. 'Maybe a fox is after dragging something down.'

The day had lost its meaning, certainly all sense of zeal; and Gethin felt that FitzGibbon's strong sense of the world, his unquestioning acceptance, was yielding now: abruptly he cried out 'Late it is, Mr FitzGibbon. Late it is. Shall we go now, before it is too late altogether?'

The effort made him tremble. FitzGibbon did not answer directly, but looked up at the sky again. A long pause, in which the dogs moved about: they would not stay down, but for Teague. The hound puppy sat close by Gethin, pressed to his leg. 'Maybe you're right, too,' said FitzGibbon at last. 'We'll just wait on Teague, and if he don't find . . .' The hound lifted its head in a howl. FitzGibbon leant over, and gave it a staggering cuff. 'Ah, you miserable sods.'

The wait drew on and on. At times Teague could be

heard, and FitzGibbon called down to him. 'Have you something there, boy? Loo into him, Teague' – a remnant of eagerness, automatic, mechanical now. The shadows darkened under the trees.

Even FitzGibbon had fallen dead silent – not a murmur of comment, no interchange, no winks, not a word of encouragement – when the dog yelled out close at hand, in the big hole itself. A roaring, rushing din immediately by them and the uncoupled terriers flew straight to the noise, the appalling furious noise. The hound puppy fled, white under the trees, and howled as it flew. Then there they were in the flying earth and dust at the mouth, all the dogs backing out: FitzGibbon on his knees, reaching far in, dragging on two terriers and roaring 'Grip to him, Teague. Hold fast to him, Cutty.' His left hand gave suddenly: the dog shot back, landing on Gethin's knees, a mess of blood and earth where its head had been. The next moment FitzGibbon reared up and backed from the hole, still grasping Teague's hindquarters and bowels.

He turned his face to Gethin; it was yellow, with the dirt and the bristles of beard showing clear. The dust died in the burrow. The appalled dogs snuffed at the blood and licked their lips, squatting tight. Over the whole open space silence came in, so strong that little falls of earth could be heard in the sett. FitzGibbon looked uncertainly from the hole to his blood-covered hand, whispering 'Bloody Christ, bloody Christ, bloody Christ.' He glanced quick over his shoulder twice, crossed himself, felt for his handkerchief and said, 'We'll get home now, if it's not too late.'

The Handmaiden

———◆◇◆———

'So it is settled, then?'

'Yes. It is settled,' she said; and since she was a woman who liked to cope with difficulties at once she stood up and walked straight to the door.

'You're not going *now*, are you?' cried Edward, in an unbelieving tone.

She turned in the opening and smiled. 'Never mind, Edward my dear,' she said, to smooth away the unhappiness she thought he was concealing. 'It really won't be anything at all. I don't mind it.'

'Oh,' he said, and there was a pause. She stood looking back, for the oh still hung up in the air, inconclusive; but all he said was, 'I was just wondering, in that case, whether you would mind coming back by the village. I am right out of tobacco. Since you will be in that direction . . .' The untimeliness of his request seemed to become more apparent as he uttered it and his voice trailed away, ending in something between a cough and a laugh, with the word 'anticlimax' thrown in.

'Of course,' she cried, keeping the surprise and disappointment out of her voice and nodding too vigorously. 'A box of Henry Clays and a yellow tin of panatellas.'

What an extraordinarily crass thing to produce, she thought, walking rapidly up the path: but perhaps he had meant to say something quite different. Perhaps this something else had turned out to be in the wrong key altogether while it was actually on its way – emotional or dramatic – and he had hurriedly substituted this awkward piece about cigars. That must certainly be the case, for no one could call

Edward blockish. How stupid not to have thought of it at the time. But that had been altogether typical of the discussion: polite, oh so considerate, ham-handed. At the very moment when they most needed to be even closer than usual they had somehow flown miles apart and had found themselves obliged to make blundering, muddled signals across the painful gulf with no common language any more.

How had it begun? And who had started it? She could not tell; but she felt the cold of loneliness and she walked faster up the hill. She had been married for more than ten years now, and she was no longer equipped for individuality: everything in what she thought of as her only genuine life had been doubled and made real by sharing, and this solitude was desolation itself. 'Mrs Grattan,' she murmured, emphasizing the Mrs: and a little later, 'I am in a silly, silly flap.'

At the top of the path she stopped, turned round and sat on a hummock. Their house lay below her, and she gazed studiously down upon it, calming herself with an enumeration of its charms: there were plenty of them, in all conscience; and once the water was piped from La Higuela there would be even more. Lawns . . .

La Higuela. She raised her eyes to look in the direction of the hidden village, and because they had been staring down for so long she saw the whole landscape with a sudden freshness – the colours all tuned sharper, the perspectives subtly changed, everything much more important. No longer blunted by familiarity, the view acquired a mysterious significance: a false significance, perhaps, but for the moment this was a portentous landscape, one that might be waiting for some huge event, the Second Coming or the Antichrist, a chariot of fire, the Annunciation.

The feeling of imminence passed almost as soon as she had formulated it; but the freshness stayed. This was how they had first seen the country: rounded bosomy little hills in the foreground, all neatly planted with almonds, precise little trees on a pink ground, like embroidery; beyond them, filling the middle distance, an ocean of olives; and then the sierra, sharp against the sky. She let her eyes run from the far left, run steadily along the deserted scene, strangely empty and uninhabited apart from the innumerable host of the olive-trees, along the crests beyond, some snowy and remote, some craggy and quite near; from left to right, taking in the ruined castle, the half-seen abandoned monastery (it had a lovely baroque court, grass-grown and silent, invisible from here), the crumbling triumphal arch among its cypresses, until she reached the hermitage. Here she paused for a moment, gazing affectionately at its little rounded apse, and then swung her head full right for the dramatic contrast, the spectacular set-piece that never failed to come off – the dazzling sweep of sea, the whole pure curve of the bay with the mountains running down to the Mediterranean at the far end, the long coastal plain, bright green with sugar-cane and checkered with different-coloured fields (they were already cutting in some places), the villages flashing white, the round walled town on its mole-hill, the Moorish fortress on the island, and all along the shore the white hem that meant there had been a storm in Africa.

This was how they had first seen it. There was the same even all-embracing light from the sun behind her, gently warm in the soft unclouded midwinter sky, ripening the bananas and the custard-apples and reflecting colour so brilliantly that she could see that the cloth hanging from a window three miles away was blue. Even the flecks of sail on the luminous sea might have been the same, unmoved.

One change there was, but it lay below her, not in the general scene: they had found the house dead and now it was alive. That made a great deal of difference, she thought, looking down on it as objectively as she could. In all this vast expanse of country there were only about seven houses visible, and two of them were ruined. A landscape had to have living houses in it (the remote toy villages of the plain did not count), and this was a living house, beautiful, reasonably-sized, deep in its own land for privacy, built round a patio and surrounded by gardens; and although from this plunging angle she could see little but its pale tiles – nearly all their pink drained out by the sun – she could place the arches of the covered walk exactly and each wrought-iron screen, each well-proportioned opening on to the outside world. The two courts lay open to her view; but so, she noticed with distress, did her little walled garden. Or at least parts of it: all the lily-bed and most of the tamarisks. They had overdone the trimming of the trees, which was a bore, because the walled garden was where she sun-bathed; and much as she liked the local peasants she had no wish to play Susannah to any yokel's elder, however picturesque. They would have a pool there, she reflected, when the water came from La Higuela, or a fountain at the very least; and what was now a tawny patch would be real grass, and Irish green.

She was above the house but no great way from it through the air, quite near enough to hear the singing. It was Conchita, of course. After a moment she attended to the song, a flattened version of a record the radio had been plugging these last months, and shrugged with a slight impatience. Conchita could sing flamenco so beautifully . . . but it was no use going on and on. She must be singing in the drawing-room. How odd. Conchita had a strong sense of the proprieties, stronger than Paula Grattan's, and she had never been heard to utter except in the kitchen or the court outside it. She *was* in the drawing-room: Paula saw the window open and a mop come out. What of it? she said, faintly disgusted at having stared so long to prove her tiny point. What *did* it matter? Yet it added a little to her returning sense of – not exactly of displeasure, which sounded pompous, but of *not being pleased*. And although she went on in a more equable state than she had started out,

this feeling came back to her more than once in the course
of her walk.

It was a damned thing, this going to La Sartén. A damned
thing. But it was no good anticipating the encounter. She
knew what she had to say, had rehearsed it several times:
why go through the whole process twice in the same day?

She walked along the sandy road through the olives,
trying to keep her mind serene and blank; and for a while
she thought she was succeeding. She took an intelligent
interest in a hoopoe that was obviously wintering here, well
north of its usual limits, a charming cinnamon-coloured bird
with black and white bars that walked busily, short-legged,
in front of her, rising every now and then to flit a hundred
yards farther on, raising its crest each time it took off or
landed; but then she found that her fingers were picking
convulsively at her balled-up handkerchief and must have
been doing so for the last half mile.

They had talked over their plan so often and for so long
now that it had come to seem quite reasonable, even quite
ordinary: no longer wildly abnormal, grotesque, impossible
to phrase with any decency. Surely, with each encouraging
the other, they had distorted their perspective? Now that
she was alone, actually walking along the cart-track to La
Sartén, with no one to prop up her conviction, the whole
thing was beginning to look to her as it must look to the rest
of the world. Or was she being stupid again?

Now that it was becoming a practical issue, a matter of
immediate action, with such disconcerting speed, the whole
thing seemed to her profoundly distasteful. An ugly business.
Was it so in fact? Was she not merely trying to shirk the
interview ahead? How much was plain jealousy?

The house came in sight. She found herself dawdling,
looking with an exaggerated interest at the olives, their
ancient trunks split, rent in three, sawed and mutilated
over the centuries, standing images of torture, confined in

round walls like well-heads, imprisoned; but each with its boughs inhabited by a luminous aerial being that lived on the wind.

This would never do. Half-consciously she checked her hair, face, clothes; and achieving a real silence of mind for the first time that day, she walked straight on through the trees.

Mrs Grattan sat on a straight-backed black chair that had been set for her where the beaten earth met the hearthstone: on her right an immense pot hung darkly over a glow in the cavernous fireplace; to her left the twilight held two or three women dressed in black: aunts. Only in front, sitting on a broken chair and two boxes was there a clearly visible group – Conchita's mother, a female cousin, and another aunt. They were all dressed in black cotton, with black shawls, black stockings, and black rope-soled shoes; they all had eyes screwed up and watering, red-rimmed from their work in the shifting glare of the olive-leaves; they were all of the same indeterminate age, between forty and eighty; and she could not certainly tell one from the other. Her chair-leg was slowly sinking where an undetected spill of soup had softened the ground, and a good deal of her attention was taken up with keeping her balance and at the same time concealing the fact; but enough was free to have received a number of impressions – the oilcloth on the round table smelt just like the oilcloth in the kitchen at Killeen: the hens that walked in and out seemed to be house-trained: the ornaments were of a fair-ground tawdriness past belief: the everyday pots were fit for a museum: they did their washing-up in what must surely be an alabaster sarcophagus. The anecdote about the health of an unknown child at a great distance was drawing to a close, and with it the period of necessarily-wasted time.

Very well, she thought, so this is it. At least I have a better lead-in than I could have expected. In an unemphatic voice she said, 'As you know, ladies, there are no children in my house. My husband and I had always hoped for a child, but now the doctors say we shall never have one. It is I who am barren, not my husband. We had thought of adoption, but you cannot tell whose child it might be; and it rarely succeeds. What we hope is to find a young woman of good character and a very respectable family whose parents will allow her to bear my husband a baby. We know that this might injure the young woman's chances of marrying, but we should provide her with a handsome dowry. We have often discussed it . . .'

Yes: very often. It was her suggestion in the first place: she had never forgotten Edward's delight at her supposed pregnancy long ago, nor the way he had sung about the house, laughing and saying 'Now we shall not all die.' And apart from that there were so many, many reasons: everything in favour of it.

And now this had seemed the perfect – not *opportunity*, that odious, exploiting word, all wrong – but rather combination of circumstances. This family was healthy, desperately poor, and manless, having been on the losing side in the civil war; they were anti-clerical and therefore not subject to the priest; the girl herself was clean, beautifully built, and now that she had been fed properly, outstandingly attractive. How brutish and ugly it all sounded: but those were the raw facts, and they were unchangeable.

Ugly. Yet in their own private language it had all become so quickly stylized, dulcified, attenuated; they had been facetious about the patter of little feet, the happy event, bawds, interesting condition, the onlie begetter.

Then again they had had one of their enthusiasms about Conchita and her family; had been silly, attributing all sorts of earthy virtues to them. Why were they both still so silly, after years and years of adult life? She did not even like these people at all, she reflected, looking at them. Those who were in the light might just as well have been in the dark:

there was nothing to be told from those closed, lined, concerned faces. Dim, dim creatures, almost extinguished by
the burden of their life. No human contact. She could not
tell what they thought of the proposal nor what they
thought of her.

Having said what she had to say right to the very end,
she sat there, physically relaxed now that the chair had
stopped sinking, but exhausted and empty. The sun, coming
in at a wider angle, lit the side of her small head, still held
up quite straight: with her ash-blonde hair and her grey
eyes, and with a composed, even remote expression on her
face, she looked incredibly distinguished; and, in that dark,
huddled room, incredibly foreign. She also seemed indifferent to the outcome of her speech.

The aunt who spoke the heaviest dialect was still going
on and on about some place of pilgrimage far away to the
north, in the Pyrenees, where childless people went on foot,
climbing the mountain to couple with their heads in a holy
saucepan: at least that was what it sounded like. She could
only be sure of understanding Conchita's mother, who
spoke something like standard Spanish.

What did they think? Many and many a time had she
inveighed against the Spaniards' stupid affectation of being
high and proud, of never smiling, of concealing their
emotions in this silly, theatrical way; often had she wished
to bang their heads together and make them behave
naturally; but never so much as now. 'They caught it from
the Moors,' she repeated, and all at once she became aware
that for some minutes past she had been driving her wedding-
ring into the knuckle of the opposing finger with painful
force. Her hands were clasped on her lap: she looked at
them. They clasped, loosened, moved over one another, and
clasped again. Dear me, she thought, I am *wringing my
hands*: so people really do: I am *amazed*.

The hoopoe was still there, drinking at a pool left from the autumn rain: it lowered its long curved beak, raised it vertically, closed its eyes and swallowed glug-glug-glug, like a hen. 'Lord,' she said, 'what wouldn't I give for a drink! A stiff one.' For a while she hesitated between the cold, roborative kick of a martini and the immediate lift of whiskey: gin was the right thing for a bawd, however, and she would have it the moment she reached home. She could see the misted glass with the olive looming faintly through and a sliver of lemon from their own untreated tree: a bowl of pine-kernels too, and some salted almonds. Conchita was very good with drinks. Edward had taught her the whole ceremony.

How astonishing that she should have come from La Sartén, thought Paula: practically a cave-dwelling. In her maid's uniform – long black dress, frilly apron, cap with streamers – she looked like a drawing from an old bound volume of *Punch*. To be sure, the clothes were natural enough in Spain, where so many things looked as though they had escaped from the nineties; but Conchita also behaved like a maid in one of those archaic pictures. You would have said she was the product of generations of good service, trained by the housekeeper of some big place in the country: she looked so much the part that it was absurd to hear Spanish coming from her mouth rather than a gentle brogue. Modest, good, and oh so pretty. It made one smile to look at her.

It *was* astonishing. But at one time she had thought it even more so: in those days she had thought Conchita quite the prettiest, brightest girl she had ever seen, and had meant to teach her to read – to bring out her innumerable latent virtues, intelligence, taste and all the rest of it. How grossly unfair, and at this point how horribly suspect, to blame the child for not being what she had never claimed to be: Conchita might be rather stupid, resistant to learning, a besotted and firmly illiterate watcher of the television, but she still remained pretty, diligent, honest, industrious, reliable . . . And she could sew beautifully, insisted Paula Grattan, topping the hill above their house, and as for washing – 'Oh my God,' she whispered, stock-still on the hidden path.

Clear below her in the small walled garden stood a figure wearing a familiar housecoat, poised there in the sun. Another squeal pierced up through the still air, and as she uttered it Conchita darted into the tamarisks. The soft branches waved; from beneath their feathery covering came another cry, the excited whoop of amorous pursuit and ritual flight. For a moment the girl reappeared at the edge of the tamarisks, struggling, the blue coat held by unseen hands in the bush, pulled open and showing her long white legs, her belly, her high young bosom. Then she toppled beneath the heaving foliage: shrill protests, diminishing; a slap. Silence.

Her first reaction was incandescent anger. She stood rigid there with her fists and her teeth clenched and all the foul words she had ever heard rushed through her mind. 'In *my* garden,' she said hoarsely. 'In *my* garden – in *my* housecoat – under my very eyes, the bitch.'

Her knees were trembling and she sat down, turning her head hard away from the garden. She scrabbled blindly in her bag for a cigarette: her face was set and very pale.

She could not light the cigarette and she threw it impatiently away. Her whole being was seething with fury and malignance: a torrent of disconnected ejaculations raced through her injured spirit: 'Couldn't wait for it – the putrid little whore – the odious, lecherous bastard – bald and fat – I always thought she was a tart – sly, sly as a cat – a cat on heat – in my own garden, the swine – turning the house into a brothel.' But all this only served to relieve her immediate rage; beneath it a monstrous suspicion was taking form, thrusting up through the anger.

How long had this been going on? Had they been making
a fool of her since the beginning? Did they do it every time
she went out? She remembered Conchita's singing 'the
moment they had the house to themselves'. But with a far
deeper stab she returned to the knowledge that Edward had
asked her to go round by La Higuela: under the stress of her
interview she had entirely forgotten about his cigars and
she was back long before they could have expected her.
Had he really done that? Had he really sent her out of the
way? She could almost swear she had seen a handful of
cigars in the box last night when she was tidying round his
chair. In that case it *was* just a pretext; his painfully awkward
words were . . . oh surely not? The mounting cold put out
her anger: her intelligence swept the declamatory nonsense
to one side and began to probe the real question. She
searched back and back into her memory: who had started
the idea in the first place? Who had renewed it when
Conchita arrived? She thought *she* had. Most probably,
though she could not remember the occasion. But had it
been planted in her mind? She wanted the truth, nothing
else at all; but it was terribly elusive. Even in this last
discussion, which had brought things to the plane of action
and which had ended so clumsily, who had been the real
initiator? Where had this dreadful lack of sympathy come
from? At one time she had thought it was from her own
suppressed jealousy; was it not really from his awareness?

Suppose he had already got the girl with child, wouldn't
he then send her off for this ghastly interview so as to have
it all legalized after the event? This was a new theory that
came forcing itself in, together with a bitter resentment of
the heartless insensitivity that *could* ask her to walk another
couple of miles after such a party, that *could* agree to her
offer to make all the arrangements singlehanded, that *could*
send her to say 'My husband wishes to use your daughter
for breeding purposes. What will you take for her virginity?'
without a scrap of moral support. Though indeed he spoke

almost no Spanish, cried another of her voices; and it was true that he – it was not fair to . . .

She brushed all that aside and with passionate concentration she burrowed through the history of words, gestures, moods, tones of voice, to find the truth; but she could not ever be sure that she had it; she could not ever be sure that she was not successfully lying to herself, either believing what she wanted to believe or insisting upon martyrdom.

She turned her head from side to side: she could not keep her mind needle-sharp and cold. She was too tired, dispirited, and sad, sad. The renewed desolation of loneliness struck her with infinitely greater force and she bowed her face into her hands: tears ran between her fingers to the dusty ground.

In time she returned to the ordinary, demanding world. She was disgusted with the scene she had made and with the poisonous, dirtying, ugly things she had said; she was disgusted with the whole thing and she was weary through and through. But while she was repairing the worst of the havoc done to her face ('My God,' she said to the little mirror, 'what a wreck') she found that her judgment had fixed rock-hard upon a decision. She would go down to the house and find out whether there were cigars left in that box or not. If there were not, if it was empty in fact, then he might just have yielded to a sudden burst of goatishness: *that* she could cope with – that would be a recognizable Edward. But if there *were* . . . why then she would have been a complacent fool for all this while. She would have been genuinely deceived and she would have to make a fundamental reassessment, since the Edward who could send her (she prayed she was not blaspheming him) on such an errand, and for such a purpose, would be a stranger to her, a man she had never really known; perhaps even an enemy. Everything she had ever heard about cold duplicity in marriage came back to her: tales of unsuspected change, malevolence, concealed bitterness.

But she had to know. She had to know one way or the other. And suppressing a little habitual whimper to Edward (her invariable recourse in unhappiness till then), she walked down the path.

Before coming to the door itself she made a noise; she was ashamed of doing so, but she had to – it would not be bearable to catch them, to stumble right on to the beast with two backs and meet its hatred. So shoving the iron garden-gate to and fro she advertised her presence: a harsh metallic clangour.

She did not know quite what she had expected, but it was certainly not the front-door half open and Conchita's face peering through the gap. Sickened by the noise she had made – the grating of the iron had pierced through and through her aching head – and perhaps encouraged by the scared little face, she walked straight forward, brushing her hands.

The girl stood back, retreating into the hall. She was still buttoning her black dress and at the same time trying to confine stray wisps of hair. She was ivory pale, and Paula Grattan could hardly make out what she was saying.

Paula's senses were unnaturally acute: she was aware that there was something here she had not expected at all, a tension in the house that did not match with her own. The hypotheses raced through her head and she was already more than half way to the answer when, glancing over her shoulder, she saw a slim youth glide away by the garden wall.

Conchita followed her eyes: stifled a despairing cry but not a flaming blush. Paula caught some distracted words about 'a cousin, who happened to be passing by', and turned away to gaze at the maiolica on the hall table while she mastered her own feelings and let Conchita do the same. Without turning round she asked where Edward was. He had gone to the village for tobacco – he had none left – had started a little after the señora – he meant to surprise her on the road.

Listening attentively to this, Paula chose her most beloved vase, the roundest, as an offering. She closed her eyes and let it drop: the pot exploded like a bomb. 'When you have swept up the pieces, my dear,' she said, 'be very kind and bring me a martini in the drawing-room. And Conchita, you must take great care with men; it is terrible what they can do to a woman.' She walked along the hall towards the door, called, 'Never mind about the drink,' and hurried out of the house on Edward's track.

On the Wolfsberg

WHEN she came out of the mindless, ruminating state that walking often induced she found that the moon had risen: a gibbous moon behind hazy cloud, but enough to flood the world with diffuse light. She also found that she had no notion where the road was going to, nor why she was walking along it so eagerly, nor indeed who or where she was.

As far as she could tell she had never seen these vast rolling mountains, with their moonwards sides gleaming a soft grey and their deep coombs as black as velvet and the white ribbon of a road that ran on and on, vanishing behind spurs and shoulders but always reappearing higher up on the next flank beyond until at last it was lost in the general merging of cloud and sky and moonlight.

'This is the damnedest thing,' she said, amused, 'I have absolutely no notion of . . .' She looked attentively at the road: it was a metalled road, but clearly few people ever used it – plants stood knee-high in the middle, and brambles reached from either side, flat on the surface. The even slope ran upwards, with no hint of its destination ahead, no high-perched village, no lights anywhere, high or low: all around the vast field of view, nothing but these soft hills for ever, limitless peace and silence; and on her right a dark mass with jagged peaks against the sky.

'I must have been lying in the grass,' she said uncertainly, picking dry wisps and fern from her clothes. 'But where? When? How come?' There was no answer at all; a vagueness like that of the grey mountains; but a placid vagueness – she was not particularly concerned or upset even when a concentrated effort brought no response.

'The great thing in these cases is not to press,' she said. 'It is like trying to force a tune – if you leave it alone, five minutes later or perhaps the next day you will find the whole orchestra booming away in your head, apropos of nothing. I have only to let a few synapses clear and I shall be able to call myself by name. I shall be able to fill out an hotel card – surname, Christian name, maiden name, date and place of birth, profession, nationality.' She walked on, whistling Death and the Maiden in an undertone, and presently she was floating along at her former steady pace.

'Amnesia, amnesio,' she sang, after a while. 'What a caper. How much is there left? A great deal, I find: speech centres unaffected, technical memory unimpaired.' She repeated the alphabet, the cranial nerves of the dogfish, the list of elements. 'I am a woman, of course; I never had any doubt of that. Youngish: sound in wind and limb.' She glanced at her hand. 'No ring: but that's not evidence. And I am *myself*, that's sure. What I am looking for is the label.' Her mind flitted away in a long digression – how much was label a component of identity? How much epoch, nationality, with all their values and associations? Take the social context away from a parcel of reflexes conditioned by that context and what remains? Something, nevertheless: the size of a dried pea or even smaller, but irreducible and enough for the statement *I am me* to carry some conviction.

'However,' she said at last, 'my sex is certain, and the time is the present, whatever that may mean: the question is, what is myself doing in these mountains?'

Here the road led her round to the westward side, still warm from the sun, and wafts of aromatic air surrounded her. 'I can't put a name to these smells,' she said, 'nor can I attach them to any sort of association: I don't know them at any level. So I must be abroad.' This reasoning was confirmed when she found a milestone by the road. 1.3 km, clear in the moonlight. 'Kilometres. So this is certainly Abroad, as I said.'

Far over, carrying a great way, there came the call of a midwife toad, repeated at solemn intervals: 'Alytes obstetricans,' she murmured; and reflecting upon the immense silence in which the sound was produced – a silence that seemed part of the moonlight and the huge expanse of shadowed mountain – she concluded that she must herself be an urban creature, used to a continual background of noise. 'Some time ago, a mile back perhaps,' she observed, 'I heard running water on the far side of the valley; and that amazed me too.'

For an indeterminate time, still walking steadily, she contemplated the peaceful infinity of rounded hills below her, the slope falling sharply from the road, and the mountains above and beyond her: it was not in any way a hostile landscape nor, though bare of trees, a savage one; but rather detached, almost irrelevant – a landscape for vague wandering rather than incisive thought. 'You would say the farther side was as clear as day,' she said, 'but when you look close everything is uncertain. The folds merge together; there is no telling where one begins and the other ends – as soft as clouds from an aeroplane. These mountains . . .' All at once she cried 'Mountains! In my very last letter – such a pompous letter – I wrote "leaving geology and everything else aside, from a strictly anthropocentric point of view, mountains are there as an analgesic." It was my very last letter to – .' And looking at them the name was almost there, hovering half-formed in her throat; but it faded, no longer to be grasped, before she could bring it to the level of perception. 'Never mind,' she said. 'I shall catch it unawares, in time.'

Yet time had lost its usual flow, and indeed almost all its meaning: that is to say, in so far as time differed from mere succession. A raucous voice from the sky startled her, breaking her train of thought — a voice that wound about, trumpeting overhead. 'Heavens!' she cried, peering up. 'What can it be? No owl ever carried on like that.' A farther trumpeting to the north, and the voice drew off to join it. Her wits returned and she said, 'Why, nycticorax nycticorax, of course. But it might have been an ostrich, judging by the row . . . Amnesia: it is an obvious refuge from distress, from an intolerable situation: everyone knows that. But I feel no particular distress; no heartbreak, no depression. Only a pleasing melancholy, engendered by this prodigious wild romantic prospect. And perhaps a sort of bruised feeling . . . I suppose,' she cried, laying her hand upon her bosom, 'I suppose I have not been knocked on the head and raped, with all that grass on my back?

'No, of course I have not: everything is perfectly intact. And I do so despise women who are perpetually being raped, or almost raped, or in situations where they might have been raped – trains, cabins, lifts, lonely woods – the lot.'

The road was turning slowly out of the light of the moon: for another hundred yards she still had her faint shadow for company, and then it was gone. In the soft darkness only the white track could be seen, and with nothing, not even moths, to distract her mind, she thought more about this feeling of a bruise. It was in her heart, and as she probed its nature it was so very like a physical pain that she could almost define it anatomically.

None of this helped her in her search for a label, but it did take away from her amusement. By the time she walked out of the darkness nothing sharp or clear had flashed into her mind, yet enough of an atmosphere in some way connected with this bruise had drifted near enough to the threshold of apprehension for her to say, 'If it is as bad as all that, I do not want to find it. Just let me walk along like this.' Another waft of scent drifted across. 'I love this road.'

The scents were extraordinarily varied; there was one as sweet as orange-blossom but far more piercing, another like pot-pourri, and one that must surely have been rosemary; and she thought she had been entirely taken up with her attempt at classifying them when she saw a piece of paper on the road.

Her automatic cry 'Let it be nothing symbolic, for God's sake. No more of those square old symbols' showed her that in fact some part of her mind had been running in quite another direction. 'No more symbols,' she went on nevertheless, 'and nothing *directed*: I have had digs enough to last me the rest of my life. If it says anything in the line of *expense of spirit in a waste of shame* I shall blaspheme.'

It was not of that nature at all. Tilting it to the best light she made out a set of diagrams, possibly directions for solving a Chinese puzzle, an interlocking wooden ball.

She opened her fingers, let it plane gently to the ground, and walked on. But the realization that some busy autonomous process had been burrowing in that direction took away the very last of her amusement: she felt an anxious, dreary expression settle on her face and she found that the elasticity had gone from her stride.

Her whistling was a failure too. 'It occurs to me,' she said, after a long course in the darkness, two miles at least, 'that the reason why I do not really care where this road is going is that I do not care where I am going either: not a damn, alas.'

Moonlight again, even brighter now; and with the change of light there was some subtle alteration in the atmosphere, the landscape and the sky – a certain air of menace. She noticed it at once, but she said, 'Nothing can threaten me: nothing can threaten me now.'

She must have reached some kind of pass, for now the road no longer climbed. After a quarter of a mile of flat it began to slope down, still in this noiseless silvery everlasting universe, the easiest road in the world to follow. And although at present the silence had something frozen and indeed inimical about it, she sank deep into its cold heart.

Down and down, so detached from her body that she could have left it to float on ahead, and so removed from any ordinary consideration that the wolf did not cause her any extreme surprise.

He was a big wolf, lean, long-legged and gaunt, and he was drifting along on the mountainside above her and somewhat behind, moving silently on a track parallel with her own. He reached the inky shadow of a rock, and she saw his eyes gleam green.

It did not surprise her very much; and although at first her heart beat hard and quick and she felt weakness in her knees, this died away and she and her pursuer moved on steadily, the wolf paying no overt attention to her and she watching him out of the corner of her eye as he loped through the clumps of thyme. Presently she heard a soft dump as he leapt down on to the road, crossed, and took up his position on her left, still a long stone's throw away, neither gaining nor losing ground.

He was easier to see now, and although the moonlight never gave a really sharp view of him at any one time, the countless glimpses built up a perfect image: he was enormously strong.

'It would be a laugh if he turned out to be no more than a prodigious great dog,' she said, and she was surprised to find tears running down her face. 'But it is more likely he is just some damned symbol, longing for a romp.'

She wiped away her tears and sniffed, and at the sound the wolf's ears pricked up. They walked on. Half a mile later she called out 'Hey!' and the wolf froze, so that she could see him perfectly: a huge brute, quite six feet long with his mangy tail; and in spite of his silver flanks he looked indescribably mean. After some repetitions of this he sprang up on to the road and followed immediately behind, his shadow clear on the whiteness; and sometimes he snuffled on her track. But she was growing bored with the wolf, bored with watching, bored with tension.

At last anger flared up: she turned and cried 'What kind of a goddam symbol are you, anyhow?' At this point the wolf was sniffing about a milestone: he kept his eye on her and deliberately cocked his leg. 'A symbol cocking its leg, for God's sake,' she exclaimed. 'I never knew wolves did that. Unless indeed it is symbol upon symbol.' She picked up a stone and walked back along the road: the wolf crouched, rigid, glaring. She called out, 'Here's for you, canis lupus,' and as her arm whipped up she knew who she was and that Hugh Lupus was an empty selfish man, hollow and false: false through and through. The knowledge came faster than the flying stone.

Bibliographical Note

———◆◈◆———

THE RENDEZVOUS: new and unpublished.

THE VALISE (formerly published as *The Walker*): *Harper's Bazaar* 1953; collection *The Walker* 1955 Harcourt Brace; collection *Lying in the Sun* 1956 Rupert Hart-Davis; anthology *The Uncommon Reader* 1965 Avon Library. The end rewritten.

THE STAG AT BAY: *Lying in the Sun* 1956 Rupert Hart-Davis.

SAMPHIRE: *Harper's Bazaar* 1953; *The Walker* 1955; *Lying in the Sun* 1956; anthology *Modern Short Stories* Faber 1964. Also German, Danish and Dutch translations and BBC third programme.

THE CLOCKMENDER: *The Walker* 1955; *Lying in the Sun* 1956.

THE CHIAN WINE: new and unpublished.

THE VIRTUOUS PELEG: collection *The Last Pool* 1950 Secker and War-burg; *The Walker* 1955.

A PASSAGE OF THE FRONTIER: *The Cornhill* 1974.

THE VOLUNTARY PATIENT: *The Walker* 1955; *Lying in the Sun* 1956.

THE LONG DAY RUNNING: *The Last Pool* 1950. Rewritten.

ON THE BOG: *The Walker* 1955; *Lying in the Sun* 1956. Rewritten. *The Irish Press* 1973.

THE THERMOMETER: *Lying in the Sun* 1956.

THE LEMON: *The Walker* 1955; *Lying in the Sun* 1956.

THE LAST POOL: *The Last Pool* 1950; *The Walker* 1955.

THE CURRANWOOD BADGERS: *The Last Pool* 1950; *The Walker* 1955. Rewritten.

THE HANDMAIDEN: *Lying in the Sun* 1956.

ON THE WOLFSBERG: new and unpublished.